"You don't think I love your brother, do you?"

Savannah asked, Cash's smile aggravating her.

"You must know by now that what I think is of little importance in this family."

"Well, I'd like to know what you think."

"People in love are always fools." Cash's amusement was gone, leaving a darkness on his features. A darkness that encouraged the doubts Savannah had been battling since her fiancé ran off. "*Do* you love my brother?"

She looked into his eyes. "I may not be a woman of passions—"

"On the contrary, Ms. Sweetfield. I think you are exactly that."

D0043115

Dear Reader,

Welcome to another wonderful month at Harlequin American Romance. You'll notice our covers have a brand-new look, but rest assured that we still have the editorial you know and love just inside.

What a lineup we have for you, as reader favorite Muriel Jensen helps us celebrate our 20th Anniversary with her latest release. *That Summer in Maine* is a beautiful tale of a woman who gets an unexpected second chance at love and family with the last man she imagines. And author Sharon Swan pens the fourth title in our ongoing series MILLIONAIRE, MONTANA. You won't believe what motivates ever-feuding neighbors Dev and Amanda to take a hasty trip to the altar in *Four-Karat Fiancée*.

Speaking of weddings, we have two other tales of marriage this month. Darlene Scalera pens the story of a jilted bride on the hunt for her disappearing groom in *May the Best Man Wed*. (Hint: the bride may just be falling for her husband-to-be's brother.) Dianne Castell's *High-Tide Bride* has a runaway bride hiding out in a small town where her attraction to the local sheriff is rising just as fast as the flooding river.

So sit back and enjoy our lovely new look and the always-quality novels we have to offer you this—and every—month at Harlequin American Romance.

Best Wishes,

Melissa Jeglinski
Associate Senior Editor
Harlequin American Romance

MAY THE
BEST MAN WED

Darlene Scalera

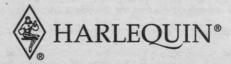

TORONTO • NEW YORK • LONDON
AMSTERDAM • PARIS • SYDNEY • HAMBURG
STOCKHOLM • ATHENS • TOKYO • MILAN • MADRID
PRAGUE • WARSAW • BUDAPEST • AUCKLAND

If you purchased this book without a cover you should be aware that this book is stolen property. It was reported as "unsold and destroyed" to the publisher, and neither the author nor the publisher has received any payment for this "stripped book."

To the Sisters of the Lake who,
when the ship was sinking, threw me a lifeline.

ISBN 0-373-16967-1

MAY THE BEST MAN WED

Copyright © 2003 by Darlene Scalera.

All rights reserved. Except for use in any review, the reproduction or utilization of this work in whole or in part in any form by any electronic, mechanical or other means, now known or hereafter invented, including xerography, photocopying and recording, or in any information storage or retrieval system, is forbidden without the written permission of the publisher, Harlequin Enterprises Limited, 225 Duncan Mill Road, Don Mills, Ontario, Canada M3B 3K9.

All characters in this book have no existence outside the imagination of the author and have no relation whatsoever to anyone bearing the same name or names. They are not even distantly inspired by any individual known or unknown to the author, and all incidents are pure invention.

This edition published by arrangement with Harlequin Books S.A.

® and TM are trademarks of the publisher. Trademarks indicated with ® are registered in the United States Patent and Trademark Office, the Canadian Trade Marks Office and in other countries.

Visit us at www.eHarlequin.com

Printed in U.S.A.

ABOUT THE AUTHOR

Darlene Scalera is a native New Yorker who graduated magna cum laude from Syracuse University with a degree in public communications. She worked in a variety of fields, including telecommunications and public relations, before devoting herself full-time to romance fiction writing. She was instrumental in forming the Saratoga, New York, chapter of Romance Writers of America and is a frequent speaker on romance writing at local schools, libraries, writing groups and women's organizations. She currently lives happily ever after in upstate New York with her husband, Jim, and their two children, J.J. and Ariana. You can write to Darlene at P.O. Box 217, Niverville, NY 12130.

Books by Darlene Scalera

HARLEQUIN AMERICAN ROMANCE

Don't miss any of our special offers. Write to us at the following address for information on our newest releases.

Harlequin Reader Service
U.S.: 3010 Walden Ave., P.O. Box 1325, Buffalo, NY 14269
Canadian: P.O. Box 609, Fort Erie, Ont. L2A 5X3

May 15
Wednesday

Savannah Sweetfield
Day Planner

8a.m.	*Two weeks to Wedding Day!*
900	
1000	*Confirm music with band*
1100	
12p.m.	
100	
200	*Meet with caterer and confirm colors on napkins—* **BLUSH**, *not pink, not peach*
300	
400	
500	

7:00 p.m.-7:30 p.m. **FIND GROOM!**

Chapter One

All of Atlanta slept except Savannah Sweetfield. Her feet, resplendent in open-toed Pradas, shoes being her one frivolous passion, click-clicked across the concrete. Her thoughts spoken into the microcassette recorder in her right fist held the same peal of purpose.

"Cathedral flowers?"

"Two dozen urns filled with larkspur and white waxflower branches, fourteen feet tall, front pew to back. Candles on metal stands ringed with lemon leaves and gardenias at aisles. Confirm white candles on altar."

She jabbed Up for the elevator connecting the underground garage to the Sweetfield corporate offices.

"Champagne?" she asked into the recorder.

"Perrier-Jouet," she answered herself.

"Crystal?"

"Baccarat."

The elevator ascended.

"Guests?"

"Double-check Grammy Eta is seated as far away from Auntie Luanne as possible. Have Cousin Charlene keep count of Great-Uncle Pom's gin fizzes.

Check on hotel gift bags for out-of-town guests. Remind—monogrammed gold W on bag or no go.''

The elevator stopped, the doors opened and Savannah stepped out, her staccato steps swallowed by carpet. All was silence as she walked through the reception area, past the offices on the fifteenth floor of Sweetfield's corporate headquarters. She was the first to arrive. Always.

The click of the record button broke the silence. ''Cocktail buffet?''

''Dungeness crab cocktail shooters, iced jumbo prawns, eastern oysters shucked to order, served on cracked ice.''

Her mother had suggested one of the wedding planners renowned in their circle, but Savannah had rejected flat-out the very idea of trusting a complete stranger with the needs and nuances of this event. This was more than a wedding. It was an alliance between old Southern stature and new South self-made standing; a merger between a Goliath of old-guard tradition and a Goliath of modern capitalism. And everybody who was anybody in Georgia had been scrambling for the right outfit and the perfect present since the day the engagement of Savannah Ainsling Sweetfield and McCormick Beauregarde Walker hit Atlanta's society pages.

Even Savannah's immediate family had been impressed enough to conceal their surprise that she would be the first of the five Sweetfield offspring to marry. She'd been born somewhere amongst three handsome brothers and a sister whose inherited beauty and charm had secured her place in the world since birth. When nothing else had developed on Savannah except her comprehension of her position in the overall scheme of things, she had realized she'd have to work harder, longer and smarter than any of her siblings just to be more than an afterthought in her family of natural wonders.

Her mother, a woman of complex and contradictory passions, had been most moved by the news of her less-endowed daughter's engagement. Once bold enough to go by train unescorted all the way to New York City to dance on the stage, Belle Sweetfield had soon found her way back to the bosom of her birth— but not before marrying a Yankee whose canny business abilities, it was politely whispered, had been supplemented by enigmatic resources. Motherhood had swiftly followed, diverting the young beauty's energies into more conventional channels and sterner standards which now, as she wept, seemed to have culminated in her daughter's betrothal to a family with land and money and pale skin and blond hair and blood as blue as anyone else's in Dixie. Savannah had even witnessed, prompted by his wife's joy, a sheen in the eyes of her father, Jack Sweetfield, a man whose fortune had given the woman he helplessly adored everything except the social acceptance she so craved.

Such was the impact unleashed by Savannah and McCormick's engagement announcement. That day, standing there before her parents' highly unlikely display of emotion, Savannah had reached for her fiancé's hand and held on tightly, suddenly humbled by the magnitude of their decision.

Not that she wasn't certain about marrying Mc-Cormick. It was just that Savannah and her intended, both sharing and admiring the same practical nature, had arrived at this juncture in a somewhat less-than-impassioned manner. They had first met as emissaries of their family's respective empires, a meeting generated by each other's desire to achieve unprecedented success for their companies, their families and themselves. Small talk had swiftly been tabled in order to discuss the possibility of the two businesses forming an unshakable conglomerate in direct response to a looming overseas threat. Savannah had known right off that her future fiancé had chosen to approach her first in the family because she was a woman. Rather than being indignant, she had appreciated her opponent's strategy—just as he'd soon learned to enjoy an equal who wasn't a pushover in the boardroom or the bedroom.

From there, the couple's remarkable compatibility began and continued into all other weighty areas. Savannah couldn't even remember who first came up with the idea of marriage. It had seemed a natural and foregone conclusion to such harmony between two individuals. After marriage, they'd agreed both would continue flourishing at the new megacompany currently in the long process of being created. Without question, Savannah would keep her maiden name, no hyphen. They'd have children eventually—two or four. Certainly not one or three—odd numbers were too awkward. And although her daddy's beginnings were farther north and a wildness had once run in her mama's blood, Savannah suspected neither she nor

McCormick would leave the South until they were planted side by side in the family plot.

She smiled as she walked down the silent hall, anticipating the jangling phones and whirring faxes and constant interruptions that would make a less-competent woman crazy. In a little under two weeks, she was going to be a wife, and like everything else she took on, she would do her job as near to perfection as possible—beginning with a perfect wedding, right down to every last petal on the thousands of sugar roses that would cover the six-foot, ten-tier vanilla buttercream cake.

Striding through her office suite, Savannah took advantage of the calm before the storm that was often her day to review her recorded checklist. She marched through the private reception area appointed by her favorite designers, ignoring the deliberately impressive sweep of the city outside the conference room's windows as she finalized the status of each detail with every exact step. She might have been stepping in high cotton by the time she arrived at her private office. She clicked off the recorder, the decisive sound making her smile. No, not one thing would go wrong with this wedding. She pushed open her office door, thoroughly triumphant.

And stopped dead for the first time in what might have been decades.

Between her two prized Eames armchairs, behind the great black rosewood desk, in her custom chair of plush gray velvet, sat a man.

A shallow breath later, Savannah's facilities snapped back into operating mode, summoning the determination and composure that had defeated many adversaries—predominantly male—before. She assessed her current enemy. Late twenties, early thirties, Caucasian but tan. Very tan. More than very tan— burnished, bronzed, a life-risking, severely glorious golden. Even at this ungodly hour of the morning when all was wan, this man was radiant. Hadn't he read the AMA reports about the dangers of excessive sun exposure? This radiance was unique, unprecedented, more than a color or a cancer-causing factor. It seemed a heat, a flare, an ignited pyre. Her climate-controlled office was, as always, a moderate seventy-one degrees, but she felt a dampness beneath the curve of her underarms, between her knees, at the juncture of her thighs.

She hated to sweat.

Preferring anger to fear, she suddenly didn't care if the brilliant male specimen before her was Ra the Sun God himself. His rear, which judging from the rest of the package was probably equally golden-brown and magnificent, was in her chair. At her desk. In her office.

She strode to the desk, grabbed the phone and dialed Security. "My office, immediately."

"Nice man, George." The sun god spoke, his tone languid, his voice warm and smoky as if fueled by the heat. She stared at him without expression. She was still sweating.

"The night security guard. His first name is George. Last name McCallahan." The man's eyes were gem-green in a face sinful in its seduction. "You didn't know that, did you?"

Even if her excessive sense of responsibility and guilt gave her the inclination, she could never know everyone who worked for the Sweetfield Corporation. "This building employs hundreds of people." Terrific. She was defending herself to a psychopath.

"His wife, Velma, is going in for a knee replacement on her right knee next week. Had the left one done five years ago. Went like a breeze. Still, George is a little apprehensive."

Play nice with the nut case now. She smiled while her mind worked overtime. Security would be here in less than a minute. Her silver letter opener could gut a catfish but it was in her top desk drawer. Still smiling, she sat down as if to have a nice chat and employed the one weapon at her disposal—she crossed her legs. While her sister had received the bulk of her mother's beauty, and Savannah had got whatever was left, her mother's dancer genes and Savannah's perverse need to exercise had eventually resulted in a facsimile of Belle's former Radio City Music Hall Rockette legs. Psychotic or not, the man was, after all, a man.

She twisted to the side, turning her entwined legs to greater advantage. If she could distract him, she might be able to grab the solid brass sculpture on the nearby table before he could stop her.

She shifted again, uncrossed her legs slowly, then recrossed them several inches higher on her thigh. The man was in a trance now. She edged her fingers along the chair's arm.

"Ms. Sweetfield?"

Savannah jumped, startled by the voice at the door.

Her arm flung out, knocking the sculpture onto her exposed toes.

Pain shot from the point of impact up her limbs. Savannah howled. She'd never howled in her life. She grabbed the murderous objet d'art off her well-shod foot and waved back the security guard as he rushed toward her.

The man sitting in her custom chair eased back and propped his long, lean legs across her polished desk. She stared at his heavy boots wriggling hello at her from the desk's corner.

"Steel toes, sweetheart. Only way to go in this big, bad world."

She met the sun god's calm gaze. In her mind's eye, she jumped up and lunged toward him, her hands circling that bronzed throat. For the first time, she wished she were a woman who followed her impulses. Her hands gripped the sculpture. "When the police arrive to take this man away," she spoke to the security guard without taking her eyes off the trespasser and his size-thirteen tootsies resting on her rosewood desk, "tell them I'll be down before lunch to personally press charges."

George cleared his throat. "Are you sure you want to do that, Ms. Sweetfield?"

Her head whipped to the guard. "A man breaks into my office—"

"Well, no, actually he didn't break in, Ms. Sweetfield."

"What'd he do—just ask for the key card at the front desk?"

"No." The security guard glanced at the man behind her desk. "I let him in."

"You let him in?" After the howl, she was careful to keep her voice temperate but firm. Her hands tightened on the sculpture.

"I figured, being the man is your fiancé and all—" Savannah's head swung to the intruder.

"And since policy had been sent down to show Mr. Walker directly to your office on arrival, I escorted him here as instructed. Had a nice chat, too."

"Well, I, for one, appreciate your rare sense of hospitality, George." The sun god spoke. "And your even rarer, although mistaken, identification of me as worthy of this lovely lady."

Amusement twinkled in the sun god's emerald eyes as he flashed the whitest teeth she'd ever seen. Had he actually just winked at her? Her knuckles popped as she clutched the sculpture.

"No, George, my brother is the lucky man who gets to marry Ms. Sweetfield. I have only come as Cupid, bringing my soon-to-be sister-in-law a message from her one and only."

"You're McCormick's brother?" The question came although Savannah already knew the answer. She'd heard enough of the stories. The one repeated most often was how he'd left his bride at the altar seven years earlier. The poor girl had died in a car crash a week later, but many said it was a broken heart that had killed her.

Savannah waited for the man to answer, the clear picture of her hands wrapped around his neck keeping her calm.

"Ms. Sweetfield, if I've—" The security guard's apology was already in his tone.

"Don't give it nothing but a chuckle, George," the man interrupted. "Ms. Sweetfield's confusion is understandable."

When had he become the one in charge? And she the one whose actions needed explanation?

Probably about the time she imagined herself bounding over the desk to throttle him.

She looked at the smooth column of his neck. Would it be cool beneath her touch? Or pulsing with the heat of life the man seemed to thrive on?

"You see, George, my name is only mentioned in whispers or paired with colorful expletives. Certainly not repeated in the presence of a lady such as Ms. Sweetfield."

"Cash Walker." Savannah's hands released from his throat. She held only the sculpture.

"Welcome to the family, darlin'." Full lips that were rumored to have kissed countless women curved with complete enjoyment. "Was it the whispers you heard or the profanity?"

She stared right back at him. There was none of the predominant refined Walker fairness in this brother. The strong, clean lines of his face were harsh and unrepentant as if they, like the man, didn't give a damn. Grooves running from his handsome nose to a mouth that seemed to say *sex* enhanced his image. His hair, the color of tarnished gold and swept back off his face with a natural carelessness, was several inches longer than her classic bob.

Her hand lifted, almost made it to her shoulder before she reminded herself that the urge to check her hair could be perceived as a sign of insecurity...or something worse.

Keeping her gaze on her future brother-in-law, she spoke to the guard. ''Yes, this is all just a silly mix-up. Thank you, George.'' She emphasized the name, to Cash's amusement.

She stood and extended her hand, keeping her gaze as firm as the shake she intended to deliver. ''Cash.'' His name made her voice sound breathless. ''When McCormick mentioned you'd be coming in early, I didn't realize he meant literally.'' She smiled a future sister-in-law's smile. ''But unusual circumstances or not, I'm pleased to finally meet you.''

He pushed back from the desk and stood. His shoulders were wide and square, his long waist tapering into an elegant V toward narrow hips and long legs. He had the lean, physically alert look of one who spent much time running. He captured her hand. She felt the thickness of his fingers, his palm's hard fullness. A man's hand. She fought to keep her grip solid.

''I hope you'll excuse my somewhat inappropriate welcome, but certainly you understand my confusion,'' she said.

Laughter came from between those curved, full lips, his eyes staying strong on her. And she knew all the things they said about him were true.

She was about to take her hand back when his head bent. With a soft brush of sweetness to her cheek, she was given a vague idea of what those lips had done to so many other women.

"Remind me never to play poker with you, Slick." A wash of breath warmed her skin.

She stepped back, ending physical contact. Her Southern manners and acquired ability to control herself and any situation allowed nothing but a gracious smile on her face and a polite hospitality to her tone.

"Please." She gestured to the circle of chairs and couch set up for conversation as well as negotiation. She waited for him to move away from her desk.

"Ladies first." The deep, thick drawl was still the song of the South, uninfluenced by his years away and his travels all over the world.

She smiled her appreciation and though the pain from her bruised toes stabbed with each step, her posture was finishing-school admirable, her steps smart as she walked to the other side of the room. She sat, crossing her legs at the ankles this time and indicated the opposite chair with her hostess smile. "We've certainly had quite a beginning. Already we share a delightful story to tell at family gatherings. Let's get to know each other further." She would be the perfect bride, the perfect wife, and for now, the perfect sister-in-law.

He crossed his own long legs and leaned back, the tilt of his lips indicating amusement and the rest of his strong, hard features naturally offering something else.

"Normally I'd be pouring you a bourbon right now, but, of course, it's a bit too early for that."

"Not by my book."

His expression gave no indication whether he was kidding or not. She suspected the latter. Still, she laughed in appreciation. Being a woman executive in a man's world, not to mention the boss's daughter, she'd encountered obstacles similar to Cash Walker and his obviously well-deserved wild-man reputation before. And she'd always won.

"My secretary will be here shortly. I'll have her bring us coffee and sticky buns. In the meantime, auspicious beginnings and delightful anecdotes aside, I must say you do aim to surprise, Cash."

"Did you expect anything else, darlin'?"

"Please do call me Savannah." She was proud of how the honeyed hospitality in her tone never wavered. "Yes, I've heard the stories. I believed about half of them."

"Believe them all."

Her smile turned real. There was nothing she liked more and found rarely than an equal opponent. "While I'm happy to finally meet my fiancé's infamous big brother, I must admit to curiosity over your early visit. I can't imagine we share a mutual fondness for rising at dawn. Certainly you don't subscribe to the early bird gets the worm theory?"

He stretched his legs out longer. "On the contrary, my fondest memories are of being in bed."

He didn't even have to add overtones. Obviously he enjoyed an equal contender also.

"Well then, since I can't imagine you forfeited any fond memory merely to meet me, I'm naturally intrigued by the timing of your introduction."

"I'm sorry if I frightened you."

"I don't frighten." She said it with a smile.

He smiled, too, as if enjoying himself. "It seems

my brother has decided to take advantage of my role as best man as much as possible and has already pushed me into service.''

She was forced to tip her head back as he stood, revealing the vulnerable stretch of her throat. He reached into his pants pocket, pulled out an envelope, and handed it to her. Her name was written on the outside.

''This was on my nightstand with a note from Mc-Cormick asking me to give it to you as soon as possible.'' The deep emerald of his eyes told her nothing.

''What is it?'' She was actually still smiling.

''All I know is I woke too early this morning— still on Central time—and beside my bed was this envelope with McCormick's instructions to deliver it to you as soon as possible.''

She tapped her fingernail against the envelope.

''He left this address, said it was the most likely place to find you. I couldn't sleep....'' He shrugged, making a simple gesture seductive.

She had several questions. *Where was McCormick? Why hadn't he just called?* Yet, even asked in the most indignant of tones, such questions would expose fear, doubt. Completely unnecessary emotions when it came to her relationship with McCormick.

''How unusual,'' she said, almost as if delighted.

She endured the man's study before he said, ''Seeing my duty's done, I'll be going.'' He turned and moved toward the door. She made no attempt to stop him.

She sat, staring at the rectangle in her hand. Finally she stood and walked to her desk, even now not allowing her steps to coddle her throbbing toes. She sat down at her desk. The chair was warm from Cash's heat. She pulled open the top drawer, removed the silver letter opener and slit the envelope. She slid out a folded sheet of good heavy bond, unfolded it, read the handwriting in straight lines across its width, folded the note exactly as it had been and slipped it back inside the envelope. Laying the envelope on the desk, she reached for the microcassette recorder she'd set on the desk earlier. She punched Record.

"Groom?"

"Gone."

Click.

HER PARENTS' red Cadillac was already in front of the Walkers' brick Georgian when Savannah arrived that evening to discuss "the McCormick matter," as the situation had been discreetly termed. She reached the library where liquor and coffee were being served along with civility, and where, at this moment, Franklin Walker was pointing his brandy at his oldest son.

"You're home not even twenty-four hours, and your brother takes off in the middle of the night without letting anyone know where he's going or for how long."

Stretched out in a corner club chair, Cash sipped his own drink, his enjoyment undisturbed. "Ironic, isn't it?"

"He did leave a note." Savannah moved into the high-ceiling room. She waved her hand to tell her future mother-in-law to stay seated and helped herself to the coffee set up on the sideboard.

"A note." Franklin's hard gaze stayed on Cash. "That you delivered."

Pauline Walker set her china cup on the coffee table only to pick it up again. "What your father is trying to say, dear, is that younger brothers often idolize their older siblings and are easily influenced. McCormick adored you." Pauline's use of the past tense did not go unnoticed by Savannah nor, she suspected, by anyone else in the room.

Cash's voice softened as he spoke to his mother. "McCormick's been a big boy for a long time now."

Wistfulness stole into Pauline's features as if she dreamed of a carefree past. A past, Savannah knew, few, including the Walkers, had been privileged to. Pauline stood as if unable to sit still any longer and smoothed her skirt repeatedly. "I won't go through this again," she announced. She moved to where Savannah stood stirring cream into her coffee.

Savannah's father, sitting near the unlit fireplace, caught his daughter's eye, raised his empty glass to her. She picked up the crystal decanter near the silver service.

"Do you know how much money is tied up in this wedding next weekend?" Jack Sweetfield asked. Savannah poured. Her father downed his drink in one long swallow. Savannah poured another. "Helluva time for your boy to take a powder." His sharp northeast accent, which twenty-five years in genteel Georgia had failed to erase, thickened with agitation. "What kind of stunt is this to pull a week before tying the knot?"

"Actually, the wedding is eleven days away," Savannah corrected.

"Do you know the money already spent for this little affair?" her father repeated.

Pauline's delicately lined lips pursed as she carried the silver coffeepot to Savannah's mother on the settee. A flush appeared on Belle's cheeks.

"Has anyone tried calling him again?" Savannah's mother attempted to direct the subject away from her husband's blunt observations.

"His cell phone is turned off." Pauline poured fresh coffee. "And he must be using cash because no charges have been reported."

"Sounds to me like a man who doesn't want to be found." Jack finished his drink.

"What if something has happened to him?" Belle wondered. Pauline paused. Her eyes, a subtle pewter shade, stared down at Belle. Savannah watched her mother's blush deepen, knew she felt raw and unfinished before the real thing.

Franklin turned to his oldest son. "If you had anything to do with this…"

Pauline laid a discreet hand on her husband's arm as she passed with the coffeepot.

Franklin eyed his heir. "What did you and your brother talk about last night when you went out?"

Cash settled back in his chair, no reaction on his face. "The Braves, the Falcons, the Broncos." He turned his far-too-handsome face to where Savannah stood. "Miss Sweetfield." His green eyes met hers as if they were accomplices. She knew he was waiting for her to look away—evidence of how little he did know about her despite his claim of McCormick's confidences.

"Did McCormick mention anything about this? Talk about taking off, getting away for a few days?" Franklin interrogated.

Cash lazily swung his head to his father. Despite his composed expression, tension burned in the space between the two men, seeming to bind them even as it forced them apart.

"We did talk about my adventures." The sarcasm was implicit. "He mentioned he'd like to travel more if he had the time, perhaps someday visit my lodge. I told him, 'Any time. Any time at all.'"

An expletive came from the senior Walker. Savannah didn't have to look at Pauline to know her lips tightened further. Instead she watched Cash's strong profile. *Don't smile,* she silently warned. Too late. The corners of that fascinatingly mobile mouth lifted.

Franklin stabbed the air with his cigar. "Tell me this, son—"

Savannah heard more sarcasm, glimpsed something raw come into Cash's eyes.

"—why would a man who has never done an irresponsible, foolhardy, childish—"

A wild torment flared in the unguarded green of Cash's eyes, then, just as abruptly, it extinguished. His gaze became cold and hard as stone.

"—thing in his life, decide to do so now?"

Cash raised his drink to his father. "Obviously it was time."

Franklin leaned down to stub out his cigar viciously, but, as he raised his head, Savannah saw where his son had learned to mask his feelings.

"The boy's probably halfway across the country by now," Savannah's father told the group. "He'll probably be shooting craps and eyeing whores in Vegas by morning."

"Jack!"

Savannah's father ignored his wife's warning. "The million-dollar question, which I'm sure the bills are beginning to tally, is what are we going to do about it?"

"Let him go," Savannah stated.

All gazes converged on her. She set down her coffee cup. "McCormick is a big boy, and if he decided he needs a few days away, maybe do something out of the ordinary by heading out in the middle of the night to some place different he's never seen, some place such as his brother's Colorado home..." She looked at Cash, trying to spy confirmation or denial but saw only a veiled interest. She turned back to the others. "The least we can do is respect his wishes. Let him go."

Belle shifted on the settee. "But it is a mite close to the wedding."

Savannah smiled at her mother. "Exactly." She smiled at them all. "McCormick is less than two weeks away from taking one of the biggest steps of his life. Is it any wonder he's acting a tad irrationally?" She paused for effect. "He's scared."

"What about you?"

Cash's question came so swift and unexpected, it might have thrown one who hadn't learned long ago that decisiveness and resolve could cover a multitude of insecurities.

"Are you scared?"

It was the first time anyone had asked her about her feelings. Feelings just waiting to waylay her.

"No," she answered with unflappable faith.

It wasn't until Franklin declared, "Cold feet," that she tore her gaze away from Cash.

"Exactly," she agreed with her fiancé's father. "Lots of people have second thoughts, last-minute doubts right before their wedding. Everyone here can probably tell me a story about a similar situation." As soon as she said the words, she realized her blunder. She swallowed hard as if to take them back. The others were discreet enough or, as she sensed in Franklin's case, disgusted enough not to look at Cash.

"How 'bout you, Daddy?" She tried to shift the focus. "You can't tell me you didn't have a moment's hesitation?"

Her father looked to where her mother sat and Savannah knew she'd made another mistake. Her beautiful mother had always been the center of her father's life, followed by his business, work, and finally, in varying degrees, his children. Savannah, with hard work crowned by her celebrated engagement, had eventually found herself fitting in there somewhere.

Her father's gaze locked with her mother's. Like many of his gender and generation, he was not comfortable with open displays of affection, but one look at the man at this moment and it was clear—Jack Sweetfield had never had a heartbeat of doubt about his marriage.

''No. Not at all,'' Her father confirmed.

An unusual melancholy rose inside Savannah. She pushed it aside. ''Exception to every rule, no?'' She smiled her most-assured smile. ''My point is,'' she sat down and folded her hands in her lap as if calm, ''when you consider the circumstances, McCormick is actually acting in a very predictable manner. I mean wedding jitters are more the norm than not, correct? So, when all is said and done, his decision to take a few days and sort everything out is nothing to worry about. In fact, it's a healthy move on McCormick's part to explore his feelings. I say, give him some time, some space, some faith, and I'll bet my favorite pair of Jimmy Choo sling-backs that two, three days tops, and McCormick will return. All demon doubts exorcised.''

Besides, she silently added her own argument conceived earlier today, *what are the chances this could happen twice in the same family?*

She didn't look at Cash as she eased back in her chair. ''After all, 'absence does make the heart grow fonder.'''

She saw the two sets of parents exchange glances. She stood, refusing to court any speculation. She picked up her coffee cup and returned it to the sideboard.

When she turned around, she saw Cash had stood also and was looking straight at her. ''Now that's all settled, time for that bourbon you promised me this morning. Ready?''

She didn't know who was rescuing who.

"Considering the circumstances, if you prefer to decline…"

Maybe she appreciated the out he offered. Maybe it was the naked emotion she had seen in his eyes earlier or the open challenge she saw in them now. Maybe it was the melancholy that lingered. Maybe, more than anything, it was her determination not to let one flicker of doubt assail her. Savannah took a step toward her fiancé's brother.

Cash showed neither surprise nor smugness, only swept his hand forward for her to precede him.

"Good night all," she said as she moved past him, attributing the unusual blitheness in her voice to her decision to keep "the McCormick matter" completely under control.

Chapter Two

Savannah had expected that Cash would drive a sleek sporty number made for speed and sin. He didn't disappoint her. The roadster was cherry-red and topless.

"Good night, Cash." She headed toward her four-door sedan—rated first in its class for safety.

"Good night?" He had thought her behind him. He now slouched against the roadster's side, recklessness meeting recklessness, and folded his arms. Every already-more-than-sufficient upper torso muscle expanded into "Body by Jake" territory.

She reached her car. "Don't worry. I'll wait until you pole-vault into that little number to make sure you don't injure any vital parts."

A thick lock of hair fell charmingly across his brow. "Mine or the car's?"

She met his shameless features. "I imagine both are extremely precious to you."

The lazy sweep of his hand as he combed back his hair was echoed by the easy curve of his lips. "You imagined right." He pushed off from the car. "So, no drink?"

She opened her car door. "You couldn't keep up

with me.'' She liked too much the sound of his laughter floating behind her. She slid into the driver's seat, careful not to slam the door and reveal her aggravation. Her first instinct about Cash Walker this morning had been correct. He was a dangerous, dangerous man.

He strolled over to her car, propped his forearms on the opened window. ''You still owe me a bourbon.''

So much for a clean getaway. She smiled indulgently. ''I don't recall ever making a definite date.''

He leaned in closer. ''I believe we just did...about three minutes ago.''

''No, three minutes ago you made up an excuse to get out of there without looking as if you were running away.''

''Is that what happened, sis?''

She eyed this man who so effortlessly elicited a rare impulse in her—to leap over any barrier and throttle him. This same man who would soon be forever linked to her as family. She couldn't decide if she should be ashamed or rueful that she hadn't acted on her first and only-ever primal urge this morning.

''You do have a pattern.''

Again, she stared at that column of bronzed flesh as if ready to reach out, take its length between her hands as if only to feel the pulse of life beneath her palms. For a woman who didn't scare easily, she suddenly was afraid.

''I'm sorry,'' she said to herself as well as to him.

He smiled. ''Don't apologize—not when you're right.''

She'd kill him yet.

"Yes, I made up the excuse, but—" He held up an index finger. "You knew it, and here you are. Here we both are. You see, I'm what's commonly known as a bad influence."

She considered her murderous instincts and the man's face too close to hers. "And you enjoy every second of it."

His smile became laughter. She couldn't remember when she'd ever heard such unfettered enjoyment. Her shoulders eased from the rolling wave of it alone. Such a dangerous man.

"That's why you won't have a drink with me?"

She realized she'd been staring at that mobile, full mouth. She stopped her own smile that had come uninvited. "Why do you want to have a drink with me?" Her voice had become as honestly earnest as his had been tempting. For a moment, the element of surprise was on her side.

"I like you."

The surprise rebounded to her, but stayed concealed beneath her dry tone. "You like me?"

"You're fascinating."

She would have rolled her eyes, but she refused to show reaction. She knew good and well she was hardly the kind of woman men found fascinating. That was her sister's department, along with the vast bevy of breathy, curvaceous beauties that after tobacco and cotton seemed to be the South's greatest crop.

She propped her chin on her fist. "How so?"

"For starters, you've been the only one not to accuse me of putting evil ideas inside my brother's head. That's as close to a defense as I'll get within a hundred-mile radius of these parts.''

She let him study her.

''How do you know I didn't tell McCormick to chuck it all and take off for the wide-open spaces?''

She looked into his eyes. ''I don't.''

His laughter was so close this time it seemed to sing inside her.

''But I don't believe in condemning a man without cause.''

''Many would say a man's past is enough cause for conviction.''

''And I would say everyone makes mistakes. I'm not fascinating. Merely fair.''

''But that's not all I find intriguing.''

She pressed her lips together and waited.

''With the wedding right around the corner—''

''Eleven days.''

''Eleven days.''

His smile aggravated her.

''Your fiancé scribbles you a note and hightails it out of town. Do you sob your eyes out, scream epitaphs or consider contacting someone named Carmine in New Jersey? No, you sit here cooler than my Aunt Raybelle's prize-winning key lime pie.'' His voice lowered. ''Fascinating.''

She sensed his observation wasn't entirely complimentary.

''So according to you, right now I should be a woman destroyed, collapsed somewhere, clutching my chest, writhing and wailing 'why me?''' she said without inflection.

He kept his voice velvet. "It would be something to see." That damn smile.

"It might amuse you—" his smile wasn't widening, was it? "—but I find such self-indulgence unbecoming." Her chin still set on her fist, she examined his extravagant features. She wasn't sure for how long—seconds or centuries. "You don't think I love your brother, do you?"

The upper hand of surprise was again to her benefit but, as before, only fleetingly.

"You must know by now that what I think is of little importance in this family."

"Well, I'd like to know what you think."

He paused a moment too long while Savannah told herself she didn't care.

"If that plucky little speech you just delivered inside was for real and you weren't just blowing smoke to buy some time before your father puts out an APB on McCormick, then I'd say my brother is a lucky man."

She smiled carefully, not wanting to reveal relief. "Or I'm a foolish woman?"

"People in love are always fools." His amusement was gone, leaving only darkness on the man's features. A darkness that could encourage the doubts Savannah had been battling since she had opened McCormick's note.

"Anything else you would like to know about me?" She was anxious to end the interview before doubts gained strength, insisted she succumb.

He didn't even hesitate. "*Do* you love my brother?"

"Land's sake, what kind of a question is that?" Even she was surprised by the anger in her response. She should look away, conceal any unwanted emotion that might come to her features, but she didn't dare.

"It seems like a reasonable question considering you're about to marry him."

She wished he'd step back from the car. "I may not be a woman of passions—"

"On the contrary, Ms. Sweetfield, I think you are exactly that."

She scanned his face but found no mockery. Despite the fact emotions did seem to come too easily when he was around, he was wrong. She was a rational woman. "You would not ask me that question if you knew me."

"But I don't know you. And you only think you know me. So, do you love my brother?"

"I suppose you asked your brother if he loved me?" she challenged.

"Sure did."

Her hands tightened on the steering wheel. He was waiting for her to ask what McCormick had answered but she had no reason to, she reminded herself. Maybe McCormick and she weren't the type to wear their emotions on their sleeves, but their consideration and respect for one another were as real as those who waxed poetic. Of course, Cash, a man so obviously ruled by his passions, could never understand such an agreeable arrangement. Naturally, he'd be compelled to question the relationship.

"I understand your concern." She was bolstered by the reasonableness in her voice. "And I find it endearing that you care so much about your brother."

His unrestrained laughter shook her to her cool core.

"Did I say something amusing?"

He actually wiped away tears. "I'm sure you've decided by now, darlin', I'm the most unendearing man you'll ever meet."

She was careful to modulate her tone. "You do have a certain gift to provoke."

"Ahh, you see…" His eyes sparkled. "I knew beneath that collected exterior there raged a wildcat."

She would end up throttling him before the night was over. "What you don't understand and have not had a chance to witness is the fact that your brother and I are a perfect match. What he wants out of life, I want and vice-versa. We've never even had one fight. Bottom line, I can't imagine anyone or anything better for me than McCormick. I'm crazy for him, totally wild, absolutely gaga."

He straightened, his laughter loose. "You've never been gaga in your life, Slick."

Why hadn't she strangled him when she had the strategy of self-defense on her side? "McCormick and I were made for each other. You can ask anyone who knows us."

He finally stopped smiling. Still she didn't like the expression on his face.

"I'm asking you."

"And I answered you." She allowed no hesitation in her voice. Yet somehow he had gained the upper hand and he knew it. "Your brother will be back in two, three days tops—"

"So you said."

"You don't believe he's coming back?"

"Again, it doesn't matter what I believe. What matters is what you believe."

"Damn straight." She imagined fierceness in her face and struggled to smooth her features. "McCormick is coming back, and we'll be married and incredibly, extraordinarily, blissfully happy for the rest of our lives." She put her car into gear but Cash didn't step away.

"Any more questions?" She called on the politeness inbred in all Southern women. She tipped her head back, matching his gaze. She didn't like the rare soft brush of her hair against her shoulders. In the silent seconds, she heard the sound of her heartbeat.

Finally he said, "Just one."

She braced herself.

"So, I won't have to cancel Dee Dee and her Dancing Divas for the bachelor party?"

She used her most executive tone. "Oh, yes, you will."

His smile returned as he chucked her under the chin as if she were no more than a child. "Good night, Savannah-Banana."

Slick! Sis! Savannah-Banana! Not to mention the obligatory *darlin'* and *sweetheart*. She watched him walk away, welcoming the relief, resigning herself to the irritation, surprised by a piddling curiosity. That's as far as she dared to delve into the emotions that suddenly seemed ready to capsize her.

He turned as he reached his car. Too late, she realized she hadn't taken her eyes off him. He rested his hand on the car's side.

"Just so you won't be disappointed."

In one smooth motion, he hurdled himself behind the wheel. He looked down, back at her, wriggled his eyebrows.

"All precious parts intact."

She fixed him with her longest stare of the night. "I don't know if I like you."

He grinned, all little boy now. "You like me."

He drove off. Probably to look for the devil himself, she decided. She headed home, vowing to dream of McCormick and that they would be wonderful dreams. Instead she found herself lying wide awake in bed, contending with the fear that had threatened to topple her since she'd opened her office door that morning. She waited and waited for sleep to come. But even counting curses against Cash Walker instead of her usual recitation of fundamental strategies for achieving success in the twenty-first century didn't do the trick.

Savanna woke the next morning without dreaming of McCormick, but the two hours sleep that had finally come were enough to restore her. With the day's new coherency and a review of her daily planner, which was always within reach, also came the realization that she hadn't told Cash about his fitting today. It was totally unlike her to be so inept. Only yesterday's unusual circumstances permitted her to forgive herself and move on to fixing her blunder. Now if McCormick were here, she could simply call him and he would see his brother got to the fitting. Problem solved. Except McCormick wasn't exactly here, was he?

She didn't allow the thought to go any further. In the day's new light, she refused to entertain any more doubts about her fiancé's untimely trip.

She'd just have to make certain Cash got to the appointment herself.

"I'M SORRY, Ms. Sweetfield." The Walkers' maid came back on the phone line. "I knocked very loudly on his door but there was no answer."

"Are you sure he's in there?"

"I heard snoring, ma'am."

Savannah released an exasperated breath as she checked the clock. No self-respecting individual sleeps until nine on a weekday. "Is anyone else home?"

"No, ma'am. Mrs. Walker just left for the salon and Mr. Walker is at the office, of course."

"And I suppose Sam drove Mrs. Walker to her appointment?"

"Yes, ma'am."

"Well, I doubt the bedroom door is locked. Just go in and give him a good, hard shake. That ought to do the trick."

"Oh no, ma'am," the other woman protested. "I couldn't do that. He's a grown man."

"So he claims." Savannah sighed again. "Listen, I'm coming right over. If, on the unlikely chance he does get up, don't let him leave the house before I get there. He has an appointment at eleven and he's not going to miss it.''

She arrived at the Walkers' three-story Georgian in record time. Still, it was almost nine-forty. She'd been up for over four and a half hours already. The most Cash had probably done in that time was roll over.

She marched in as soon as the front door opened. ''Which room is he in?'' she asked the maid as she started up the stairs.

''Second floor, fifth door on your left, ma'am.''

Savannah reached the second-floor landing and strode down the hall to Cash's room. She rapped on the door loudly. Without waiting for an answer, she twisted the knob. By the time Cash showered and dressed, they'd be lucky if they made the appointment on time.

''Cash?'' She announced herself to the lump burrowed beneath the bedcovers. She marched to the window and threw back the curtains. She turned, triumphant. Still no sign of life from the bed. She marched to the bed, put her hand on what she presumed was a shoulder and gave it a good shake. ''Cash, get up now.''

With a groan, he rolled over. His eyes still closed, he warned, ''You're gonna pay for that, Angeline.'' Grabbing Savannah's hand, he pulled her down onto the hard heat of his body.

Her mouth opened, only to be covered by his, his hands capturing the back of her head, thrust into her hair, holding her fast. He crushed her lips beneath his own, the kiss hot, urgent as if he'd been waiting his whole life for her. Shock, outrage and a sudden sense she had never been kissed before filled Savannah. Her anguish seemed to fall, matter no more beneath a passion and, heaven help her, a pleasure spreading, flowing through every inch of her, striking her senseless.

She squirmed, but her movements, the friction of muscle and flesh, were desire's dance. An unintelligible plea came from the back of her throat, but Savannah could no longer be sure for what she begged. Her efforts had eased her lips wider, unwittingly provoking that hard, wonderful mouth deeper. She tasted a wildness, the sting of uncontrol. She stopped squirming. Her hands fisted against the sides of the body blanketed beneath her, against the heat, the power, the scorching need.

With a fierce twist of her head, she wrenched her mouth free. She held the breath that would come out as a gasp.

"You're in bigger trouble now." His hands reached for her once more.

"Cash!" she snapped, an inch from his face.

He opened his eyes; she filled his vision. "Whoa!" His head jerked back, surprise taking all the hooded sensuality out of his features. She wanted to jump up and run from his provocative power searing her body. She didn't move. She'd be damned if she'd give him the satisfaction. It was too late anyway. She'd known his kiss, even though it had been meant for another and meant nothing. Yes, that was the thought she would cling to when the memory came.

She tasted her lips. "I see you had that drink after all last night."

Amusement moved into his features. The sensuality

had already returned. "You should have come with me, Savannah-Banana."

"It's a regret I'll learn to live with." With as much dignity as possible, she rolled off his body and rose from the bed. She looked down at him with perfect composure. "Get up and get dressed."

He shrugged. "Okay, but I've got to warn you I sleep in the nude." He started to push back the covers.

"I already knew that." Savannah moved to the door, adjusting the starched collar and cuffs of her shirtwaist, as his rich laughter came. "You have a fitting at Mr. Max's Formal Wear today. We're to be there in less than an hour. I've never been late for an appointment in my life and I don't intend to start now." She walked from the room without another look at him.

He sank back against the pillows as the door closed, Savannah's sweet taste and soft warmth still holding him like a dream. He had drunk too much last night for the first time in many years. Yet it was also the first time he'd been home in many years. A throbbing ache began in his head. He closed his eyes, but not to relieve the pain. No, he welcomed the pain. He closed his eyes to wipe out the memory of the moment that had just happened. Desire only strengthened. He opened his eyes, everything too real. He had wanted Savannah. He had touched his lips to hers and tasted the sweetest of promises. He threw back the covers and swung his legs over the side of the bed. He shook his head. "Hell." He laughed again, this time at himself as the need clutched him.

Savannah made it as far as the second stair before she gripped the rail to steady herself. Still, sensation overwhelmed her. Every boundary she'd ever crafted seemed to have dissolved, leaving her vulnerable. It'd been the surprise, the shock, that's all, she told herself. Nothing more, nothing more. Still the urgency rose.

She watched him come down the stairs twenty-five minutes later. "You forgot to shave," she noted.

He smiled at her. "I didn't forget."

"I hope you at least brushed your teeth." She turned to the door.

"Why? You gonna kiss me again?"

She spun around, angry with him, even more furious with the desire spiked by the mere suggestion. "You kissed me."

"You kissed me back."

"A gentleman wouldn't—"

"Now you're flattering me, Savannah-Banana."

She forced her expression bland. She didn't have to tell him how much she hated nicknames. She had the feeling he already knew.

"We keep going the way we are—" he still smiled "—and soon we'll have a whole repertoire of anecdotes to share at family functions."

Her hand sliced the air, dismissing him and his efforts to infuriate her. She yanked open the door. "Let's go. I don't want to be late."

"Why?" He tripped down the porch stairs, easily catching up to her. "They'll force us to wear pink cummerbunds?"

"Actually, they're peach." Savannah pulled open the car door.

Cash stopped dead, such a look of alarm on his face, Savannah would have smiled had it been anyone else.

"You're kidding?"

She looked at him, confused. "They match the bow tie."

She slid into the driver's seat, enjoying a smile until Cash slid in beside her.

"You are kidding," he decided.

She glanced at him, her expression betraying nothing. "Buckle up." She put the car into gear and headed for the interstate.

"Stop." He pointed to a mini-mart as they came to an intersection "I need caffeine."

"There's no time."

"Come on." He elbowed her in the side as if they were old school chums. "A man can't live on love alone."

She had an urge to rev the engine and shoot past the convenience store, but she always drove at the speed limit.

He leaned back against the seat, stretched his arms, reducing the space even further within the car. "If you're in such an all-fired hurry to get downtown, why are you driving so slow?"

"I'm driving at the posted speed limit." She snapped on her blinker, eased into another lane.

"Follow all the rules, don't you, Slick?"

"That's what they were made for, Walker."

"Maybe, but it's more fun to break them."

"There's more to life than fun."

"Is that what you want on your tombstone?"

She decided to ignore him. In reality, she was too aware of him—his size, the movement of muscles as he shifted in his seat. The omnipresent heat, seductive as a southwest wind. Heat that she'd told herself she'd only imagined, until this morning when she'd felt it with her own body.

Fortunately they weren't far from the heart of downtown now, having left behind the old-money estates and new-money monster mansions. Mr. Max's was north of the city's center among the upscale department stores and towering hotels and office high-rises. Cash groaned as they passed an advertisement for Fresh Mountain Roast Coffee.

He slumped against the seat. "All I can say is the bridesmaids better be gorgeous—each and every one of them."

Savannah thought of her sister. Cash would be pleased. "I'm assuming then, you're not bringing someone to the wedding?"

"Why? Do you need a date?"

Patience, Savannah, patience. "You just seemed rather fond of this Angeline person—"

"Angeline?"

The unexpected steel in his voice drew her gaze. His expression was even harder.

"That's the name you called me when you accosted me in your bedroom. I assumed—"

"Honey, I've done a lot of things in a bedroom but accosting has never been one of them."

As usual, his recovery was swift. Jaw set, she focused her attention on the traffic.

"You're thinking you don't like me again, aren't you, Slick?"

Her jaw muscles locked.

"Angeline was the woman I left at the altar seven years ago."

She swung her head to him. He was watching the passing buildings, the streets busy with people. "I'm sorry."

He angled his head to look at her.

"Really, I'm sorry. I didn't know. I mean I knew what happened but, but—" She was actually stammering.

"The story isn't exactly the type of fare that lends itself to amusing anecdotes at family reunions, is it?"

His barbs were rendered null and void by the pain etched in his expression.

"Why'd you do it?" Her words came without thought. Blame it on her current situation. Blame it on the loneliness she sensed beneath his laughter. She needed to know.

He shook his head. "She knew it was over. I had told her that morning."

"Maybe she didn't believe you?"

His words were certain. "She believed me."

Savannah sensed he would say no more. She tried to fill in the blanks. "You were scared?" She felt her own fear, refused to let it take hold.

"Not at all. I wasn't scared of anything back then. I was gaga about her." He winked at her. She had to smile, her own fear falling away.

"Wild about her, absolutely wild. Followed her around hot as a three-dollar pistol." His smile was rueful as he looked out the windshield at nothing and remembered. "It ended badly, but boy, in the beginning…it was something."

Savannah could only nod dumbly while a faceless, nameless need rose inside her as if she were twelve again, dreaming of her first kiss. She wanted to ask more, know everything, but Cash turned to the window, his face lifting toward the bronze sunlight. "I hate this damn city," he said.

She returned her attention to the road, started to search for parking. "They always have coffee for the customers at Mr. Max's. Mr. Max insists it be brewed fresh on the hour, every hour. The beans are hand-ground." It was all she could offer him at that moment.

She felt a warm gratification when she heard his chuckle.

They were ten minutes late for the fitting but no one minded except Savannah, and even she had ceased to care at that point. Cash immediately christened the owner Max the Madman and after two cups of black coffee with what Savannah thought was an excessive amount of sugar, he charmed the rest of the store's personnel. Savannah watched him, wondering if anyone, even those who knew better, walked away from him untouched?

When he stepped from the dressing room, in classic black that instead of refining him only made his raw maleness more lethal, the assistants oohed and aahed, and even Savannah had to swallow hard twice. But when Mr. Max turned to her to second his opinion of Cash as ''the most handsome best man to ever set foot in Mr. Max's Formal Wear,'' Savannah merely looked at Cash and in a bored tone, asked, ''You will shave for the wedding, won't you?''

Chapter Three

Savannah didn't see Cash the next day nor the next, but when she opened her office door on the third morning, she found him once more behind her desk. She didn't even miss a step as she walked into the room and was thoroughly pleased with herself.

She smiled cordially. "How's George doing this morning?"

The amusement increased on Cash's face as if he enjoyed her. "Not bad."

She set her briefcase on the desktop, sat in the chair opposite. "Still worried about Velma's knee, I imagine?"

Cash nodded. "But his daughter is coming in from the west coast day after next for the operation. He's happy about that."

Savannah arranged her hands in her lap. In the last two days since she'd seen Cash, she'd decided his sole aim was either to incense or entice. So realized, his efforts lost all power over her.

"His daughter lives quite a ways away." She could play.

"California. Married not long ago. Nice fella. Lawyer. George's other daughter works in Seattle, married three years. Her and her husband made a killing on an upstart dot-com company two years ago.''

"I'll bet George and Velma are campaigning like mad for grandchildren then.''

Cash smiled, a smile not made for morning but for night and smoky music and the beat of something rare in the air.

Savannah gave him a polite half smile she knew suffered in comparison. ''A second bright and early morning meeting in the same week? You keep up this ambitious schedule, and you're going to ruin your reputation.''

"Or yours.''

Her gaze stayed steady. ''Do tell, Walker, what brings you out once more at this unusual hour?''

"McCormick called me last night around 1:00 a.m.''

She was grateful to be sitting down. A thousand urgent questions rose. She refolded her hands, waited for Cash to continue.

"He's at the lodge in Colorado.''

She seized this small satisfaction. ''When is he coming home?'' She was thankful there was no shake in her voice.

"He didn't say.''

"He didn't say?'' Still she kept her voice even, her gaze level. ''What *did* he say?''

"He's conflicted.''

"Conflicted?'' Her voice sounded foreign, her world suddenly held together by precarious threads. She sat very still and stared at Cash, afraid to shift her gaze and set off an avalanche. The colors of his eyes tempered. He knew, she realized, had learned a long time ago—all is nothing but shifting sands, winds of fate. It had been the birth of his wild heart.

She pressed her sweating palms against the smooth surface of her skirt as she stood. She moved to her briefcase upright on the desk and opened it. Cash watched her.

She removed several files from the case and piled them on the desk. Plucking a pen from the silver cylinder on her desk, she set it before Cash. He looked at it curiously. She ripped a piece of paper from the notepad next to the pens and slid it toward him.

"I'll need directions to the lodge from the Denver airport." She riffled through the papers in her briefcase, leaving those that could wait, removing those that would have to be brought with her. She would give her tapes, along with detailed instructions on what needed to be done for the wedding until she returned, to her mother and her assistant.

Cash tapped a rhythm on the desk with the pen. "You're going out to Colorado?"

"I'll fly out on the company plane, I hope by noon." She slapped another folder onto the pile. "One, two, at the latest." She glanced at the blank sheet of paper before Cash. "Just give me the lodge's name. My secretary can get me the directions."

The beat of the pen stopped. "You know what you're doing?"

"Always." She lied.

Cash crumpled the paper in his fist. "I'll drive you up to the lodge from Denver."

She looked at him across the wide desk. "Not nec-essary. I'm perfectly capable—"

"That I don't doubt, Slick, but the only reason I came back here is for my brother's wedding and—"

"There'll be a wedding."

He nodded, agreeing although she suspected he was humoring her. "At that time, I'll come back, put on a monkey suit and do the Macarena until there's no more booze or pretty ladies left."

He stood, shot the crumpled paper into the waste-basket. "But until then there's not much reason for me to be hanging around."

"Did you know he was in Colorado?" She doubted he'd tell her the truth, but she wasn't convinced he would lie either.

He stood so much taller than she and much too sexy a man for early morning. McCormick was her height, never giving her the need to toss her head as she did now, letting her hair sway, her throat lengthen.

"I'm not the enemy, Slick."

He wasn't an ally either. They both knew it.

He went to the door. "Listen, I've already made plans to go back to Colorado today anyway. If you want to fly out together and I'll drive you up the mountain from the airport, leave a message at the house with the flight's time and where I should meet you."

"There'll be a wedding," she felt compelled to say one more time although he was already gone. She listened to the low murmur of his voice, the answer-ing laughter of her receptionist, who for the first time in her career must have come in early. Savannah's sense of a world upside-down increased.

"There'll be a wedding," she muttered, returning to her reports. "So prepare to macaroni, Walker."

SAVANNAH COUNTED five rows back, neither too near the front of the cabin nor too far back. She took out several reports and her microcassette recorder from her briefcase before stowing it in the overhead compartment. As soon as she sat down, she buckled her seat belt, adjusting it around her hips, leaning forward to check for minimal slack. She straightened, rattled the seat back, then the ones to either side of her, making certain all were locked in position. Next she checked the latches by giving all the trays in front of her a firm tug. All appearing secure, she evened the pile of reports on her lap, clutched her recorder and bent her head to review the figures on the top printout.

Cash plopped down in the seat next to her. His weight involuntarily swayed her toward him. His body was too big beside her in such narrow seats. Savannah focused on the report. Cash reached up to the overhead controls, flicked the lights on, off, twisted the air vents all the way open. The reports on Savannah's lap fluttered.

"Cash." She slapped her palm on her papers as they prepared for liftoff.

Her head came up. An air stream blasted her full in the face. She jerked back. She reached up and wrenched the air nozzle closed.

"Fresh air. Very important when flying. Cabin air

can be very drying. Plenty of liquids is good, too.'' Cash reached toward the nozzle.

Her hand clamped his wrist. ''I'll take my chances, thank you.'' The strong beat of his pulse pressed against her fingertips. She let go. She looked pointedly around the empty cabin. ''You do realize we're the only passengers.''

''Are you flirting with me, Slick?''

She meant to count to ten, got as far as five. ''Wouldn't you be more comfortable in your own row where you could stretch out, take a nap or do whatever you do?''

He smiled but didn't move.

''I have work to do.'' She returned to her report, clicked the recorder to make a note.

He propped his elbow on the armrest and leaned over to scan the report on her lap. His arm pressed against hers. The fine hairs of her flesh might as well have been exposed nerves.

''Let's see what we've got here. A Second Quarter Departmental Survey on the Effective Utilization of Potential Product Preferences,'' he pretended to read, ''as Defined by Targeted Consumer Dynamics within the Mid-Atlantic North American Quadrants Including but Not Excluding Those Market Bases—''

''Okay, okay.'' Savannah snapped off the recorder. Her other hand gestured surrender, and let her slide her arm away from his. ''You talk the talk, Walker.''

''Please. You'll make me blush.''

''McCormick said you had a brilliant business mind.''

"Merely an example of that 'younger sibling' infatuation championed by my mother the other night."

"McCormick said you were a natural—much more so than he could ever expect to be."

"I was the oldest son. My father had annual reports read to me while I was in utero."

"What happened?"

He made his features into a stern mask. "I was a grave disappointment." Pain flashed in his eyes, belying the doomed baritone of his pronouncement.

"Seven years is a long time."

He rested his head against the seat. "Depends on your perspective, Slick."

"And what's your perspective, Walker?"

He inclined his head to her. She saw the amber and gold in his green eyes.

"That a lifetime isn't long enough, Slick."

She studied his face for an extra beat before turning to her papers.

"You ever fly, Slick?"

She wasn't going to get any work done. "Of course."

"How 'bout fly the plane yourself?"

"Be the pilot?" The alarm in her voice gave him his answer. She tried to focus again on the figures in front of her only to sigh and raise her gaze to him. "I suppose you have?"

"Flew my first solo about five years ago."

The idea of voluntarily putting your entire existence thousands of feet in the air was incomprehensible to her. "Why?"

"Why?"

"Why'd you learn to fly?"

"Simple. Because we're not supposed to." He smiled the smile that forced her to stare at him.

"Not supposed to what?"

"Man's not supposed to fly."

"I agree with you there." She returned her attention to the numbers on her lap.

"Yet we do. Some buttons, some fuel, a machine and, there you be. Breaking all kinds of natural laws. Man just can't resist."

She drew up, looked aghast as his strong arm reached a breath away from her breasts. He slid up the shade on the small side window that she'd purposely left closed.

He settled back in his seat. She breathed again. "Shouldn't be at all." He smiled at the patch of view exposed by the side window. "Moving above the earth higher and faster than you ever dreamed, steering right into the clouds, coming out above them. The light like heaven."

She turned her head to the window, but she didn't see what he saw.

"Everything else falls away. The boundaries, the shoulds, shouldn'ts, everything you thought you knew, thought you understood…no more." He leaned his head on the seat, closed his eyes. "Then comes the big trick when you're up there among the clouds and the light, and you have to make yourself think you're in control when you now know you have no control at all. And never really did. No one does."

He was quiet, and she thought him done. Still she stared at him.

"What's it like?"

His eyes stayed closed. "You're scared beyond imagination, beyond everything, exhilarated, sweating and feeling as if you've never tasted one pure breath until that moment. You ever feel that, Slick?"

Once. She was unable to look away from his face. *When I opened my office door four mornings ago and found you.* The fear washed over her as frightening as it'd been the first time. His eyes opened.

She had been afraid then. She was afraid now.

"No," she lied.

"Nooo?" He repeated the word with a sad drawl. "Never? Not one moment when everything became confusion and chaos yet so clear and real you didn't know if you wanted it to end or to go on forever?"

She shook her head.

"Not even when you fell in love?"

"Love?" She declared flatly. "Sounds like lust to me."

He tipped his head back and laughed so boldly she found herself smiling.

"Ms. Sweetfield?"

The assistant pilot stood at the front of the cabin. Savannah stopped smiling as if she'd been caught doing something wrong.

"We're number two in line for takeoff."

"Thank you."

The assistant disappeared back inside the cockpit.

"Bet you don't know his first name either?"

Her eyes met his of emerald. "Are you going to move or am I?"

"Stan." He rose to plop into the row directly

across from her. He reclined, sprawling his long legs out into the aisle. "How's this?"

"You should put your seat in an upright position." Savannah tucked the microrecorder into her purse, made sure her cellular was turned off.

"Did you turn your cell phone off?"

Cash shook his head. "Don't have one."

"You don't have one?"

"Hate the damn things. Reception doesn't work half the time in the mountains anyway."

Savannah set her paperwork on the floor underneath her seat, placing her purse flat on top. She checked the trays in front of her a final time. "Law, I couldn't survive."

"It's a primitive lifestyle, but I've adapted. Man versus nature and all that, you know."

"Yes, you've got that caveman mentality about you."

She didn't hear Cash's reply. The plane began to taxi. She clasped the armrests, braced herself against the seat.

"Ahhh, my favorite part," Cash declared.

She glanced over. "Put your seat belt on."

The plane moved forward.

"It starts so slow, you don't think its ever going to happen." His voice was like poured wine.

"It becomes stronger little by little. The power, the strength surrounding you, building, starting to surge." The plane gained speed. "Faster and faster."

As if in response, the plane quickened. Savannah tightened her grip on the seat's arms. The air outside began to moan.

"No more than wind now. On the edge. Not here. Not there. Unable to know if you can stand it." All was Cash's voice and the scream of air and the assault of speed.

"Deciding it can't happen, it can't be possible." The plane heaved. "One last thrust." Anticipation swelled Cash's voice. A final jerk of metal and defiance slammed Savannah into her seat. The plane lifted.

"And you're flying," Cash sang out.

Savannah grabbed the bag from the pouch in front of her and threw up.

"Slick, you okay?"

She shot him an angry glance only to find him leaning across the aisle, offering a wad of tissues. She grabbed them, waving him away, then bent toward the bag as round two began. His weight was again beside her, the tentative pat of his hand on her rounded back.

"Go away." She wiped her mouth with a tissue, threw it into the bag.

"Don't like flying, do you, Slick?" His fingertips rubbed a light circle between the broken wings of her shoulder blades.

She patted the beads of sweat from her forehead, her upper lip. "I prefer my feet on the ground."

She couldn't help but appreciate his chuckle. "Now why doesn't that surprise me?"

She glanced sourly at him. He patted her back.

"You should have your seat belt on," she scolded, then twisted her head away. Oh no, round three.

WITH THE TWO-HOUR time change, the plane landed at Denver International Airport at almost the exact same time it had departed Atlanta, a fact that gave Savannah an odd comfort. The plane was needed back in Atlanta tomorrow but would layover at the airport for the night. Savannah would call in the morning to say if there'd be passengers or not. She was not leaving Colorado without McCormick.

''You ever been to Colorado, Slick?'' Cash maneuvered out of the airport's parking garage.

''I was at a seminar at the Brown Palace Hotel two years ago.''

''You've never been to Colorado then.'' He turned right as they left the airport and onto the interstate heading west. At first, Colorado was only the endless tangle of traffic, the flat suburban sprawl, the strip shopping centers that surrounded all major cities. But when, worn from the flight and feelings, Savannah closed her eyes, she found the strong gold light of the western sun dancing beneath her lids. When she opened them, the city had fallen away and the Jeep was angling upward as if she and Cash were about to take flight again.

They moved into the mountains, the roads becoming as narrow and sharp as the terrain they traced. One-eighty curves were announced by no more than the bright display of an upside-down *U* on shivering signs. Still the turns leapt up like gleeful gremlins before twisting into the mountain's blue shadows.

Up they climbed, the high wall of gray and green always beside them, so vast and close, the evergreens seemed to lean over the car. Yet Savannah only turned her head and there was nothing. No more than air and rusting guardrails angled toward the road's edge as if in homage to the abrupt drop beyond. They climbed, the air becoming finer, lighter, bringing a dizzying clearness to the hard edges, steep planes. Here was none of the slow liquid heat of the South.

They turned off the interstate and moved straight into a deep V of green. Along the way, Cash pointed out various places, points of interest, but Savannah spoke little. When she did, it was a near-whisper, as if the mountains' silent presence was already as strong and deep as a beat in her blood.

Cash made a sharp left turn onto an unpaved road snaking into the aspens and pines. At the corner, Savannah spied a propped half log. On its smooth side, Lost Ridge and an arrow were hand-painted in white. For a mile or more, the Jeep bumped along through untamed growth, climbing and dropping, until the green suddenly broke into a clearing blanketed with red, yellow and purple wildflowers. At its end was a towerlike structure with a clutter of vehicles and equipment in various stages circling its base. Several golden dogs came bounding toward the Jeep as it passed.

The raw road threaded past a dozen scattered homes of weather-darkened wood or thick logs, some one-story, others two, all with wide porches and many unshuttered windows. Farther on, set low as the land dipped, a cluster of buildings sat closer together, crowned by the bell tower of a simple white structure. ''Downtown Lost Ridge,'' Cash noted.

The vehicle veered away from the town's center

onto another dirt road that fell rapidly only to climb until it crested a flat plain. There, clinging to a hill's steep side as if suspended in a sea of this magic mountain air, was a large, sprawling lodge.

Cash parked, turned off the engine, gazed out the window a moment as if, like Savannah, seeing everything for the first time.

"The town was originally a ghost town like others after the mines closed, but was re-incorporated in the 1980s to create the zoning to keep the growing ski resorts from coming in."

She followed Cash up the wide timber steps to a long, split-rail porch.

"There's about fifty of us. Homesteaders come and go. Population swells during ski season." He opened the front door, inviting her to enter.

She stepped into a sense of immense, unbroken space. The first floor seemed one wide-open room swirling around a massive stone hearth stretching high to the cathedral ceiling's great beams. Everywhere light leapt and danced, splaying from the wall of windows to bounce off the burnished floorboards onto the glossy log walls and the copper lamps hanging above. Fire moved golden like a great wind in the hearth. She imagined a couple entwined before it in the dark, a woman's head resting on a man's shoulder, his arms wrapped tightly around her, his cheek on her hair. What a shame she and McCormick couldn't stay here longer to celebrate the end of this odd journey. Perhaps, if they were careful with their respective schedules, they could return here next year. An anniversary celebration.

Pleased by her idea, Savannah crossed the jewel-toned Indian rugs past the sea of outsized sofas and chairs to the wall of glass. Even inside this world of light, the mountains reigned.

She felt almost lightheaded as she heard a door open on a far wall behind her. "McCormick..." Her voice came musical and unexpected, her head dizzy with the knowledge that it was almost over. Her long, unexpected trip was about to end. She had found her fiancé, and she no longer worried about his hesitancy to come home. How could anyone be expected to be rational here where logic dwindled and practical thought took flight as the cliffs climbed and the air thinned?

She turned to the opening door. Her fiancé's name was still on her lips as she was struck by the image of a huge, dark man, the reflected light and shimmering radiance making him seem larger and darker than humanly possible. His skin was the color of unpolished brass, bronzed not only by sun but by soul. His face was noble-boned and ancient as if carved out of the same earth as the mountains around them.

"Hello," she said, the shock not altogether unpleasant, not even unexpected in this place of wild, primitive beauty.

"Hello." A smile split his rawly handsome face, a white grin so disarming in all that darkness that Savannah smiled back wide, feeling she was spinning once more.

"Savannah, this is Thomas White Calf, but everyone calls him Mountain."

Savannah saw that beneath the older man's heavy

thick brows, his coal-black eyes danced with light. "An apt nickname, to be certain." Her voice had never flowed with so much music of the South. She stepped toward the apparition of a man to offer her hand, and a lightness came to her limbs. She might have laughed, the man was such an inverse image of her fiancé. Yet she remained undaunted. She would find McCormick in this strange land where neither one of them could stay.

"Mountain, this is Savannah Sweetfield."

"Savannah Sweetfield." Her name came exotic from between his bronzed lips. She smiled wider for no reason at all.

"I'm McCormick's fiancée."

He nodded, his study full and complete upon her, and Savannah, in all this radiance and wildness, was not self-conscious at all.

"Is he here?"

Those ancient eyes looked away from her to Cash. "Didn't he call you last night?"

"Woke me up around 1:00 a.m. without so much as an 'I'm sorry,'" Cash grumbled.

Mountain's gaze fell on Savannah. For the first time since she'd stepped into the lodge, she felt the weight of her own body.

"Where's McCormick?" The gravity came back to her voice, too. Her limbs felt heavy as grief.

Even the silence had weight, now broken only by a single word sounded like the toll of a bell.

"Gone."

Chapter Four

"Gone?" Savannah spun around to Cash. "Did you know about this?" If he smiled, she *would* strangle him this time.

He shook his head and saved his life. "He didn't say anything to me."

She wasn't sure whether to believe him or not. She huffed for good measure, trying to catch the truth in his eyes. She saw only the confusion she felt.

"When did he leave?" Cash asked Mountain.

"First thing this morning," the large, dark man said.

"Where was he going?"

"South."

"Home?" Savannah's voice filled and was again rich. "Law, he probably was landing in Atlanta as we were taking off." Her relief released in laughter. "Doesn't that beat all?" She smiled at Cash, forgiving him everything. He didn't see her smile. He was looking at Mountain. She followed his gaze.

"Farther south than Atlanta, ma'am."

"I don't understand." She kept smiling as if a

promising curve of the lips was all it took to hear the answer she hoped for.

Mountain's gaze darted to Cash. Savannah smiled like an idiot. "He was talking about Mexico."

"Mexico?" Savannah whirled around to Cash, saw the surprise on his face. Still her confusion needed venting. "I can't believe he didn't say anything to you about this!"

"Mexico?" Cash's voice only held mystery.

Savannah felt unsteady, as if everything were shifting, slipping away from her.

"Oh, for the love of my Grammy Eta." She plopped into the nearest seat, afraid if she kept standing her knees would buckle. She wouldn't let anyone see her fall. "Doesn't McCormick know you go on honeymoon the week after the wedding, not the week before?"

She allowed her head to drop along the couch. "And you take the bride with you." She listened, amazed, as the laughter rolled out of her and mingled with the light.

Cash eyed the woman, long and lean along the couch, her laughter sounding crazily free and girlish. He could almost see the child she might have been. He heard that little girl's fear.

McCormick had told him of Mexico the first night Cash had arrived in Altanta. McCormick had gone there on business, but his talk had echoed of pleasure. He'd spoken of a woman, but only fleetingly, as if she'd been no more than a vision glimpsed, then gone, in the marketplace. It didn't seem like his brother to go running after a dream. There must have been more between McCormick and this woman he spoke of with a lover's look.

Savannah's laughter lessened to a simmer. Mountain watched her with concern. She would despise any sympathy. "It's the altitude." Cash allowed her to save face.

Mountain nodded. "Gets them every time."

As Cash suspected, in his friend's eyes he saw there was more to be told about McCormick and his sudden wanderlust. "Is he okay?" Cash had to know.

Mountain glanced again at Savannah. "He seemed troubled."

With a hiccup, Savannah's laughter ended. *"Conflicted?"* She sat up straight. As easily as she'd taken to laughter, she now sobered. Cash's worry increased. This crazy female was beginning to get under his skin, and he didn't like it.

"Yes," Mountain agreed.

"And the answers to his problems can be found in Mexico?"

Mountain hesitated as if unsure what to say.

"Many others before McCormick have thought so." Cash came to his friend's rescue.

"Not the week before their wedding, they haven't," Savannah snapped.

"You'd be surprised." He grinned, pleased by her piercing glare. Who'd ever have thought he'd be happy to see Savannah back to her normal uptight, self-righteous self?

"Why did McCormick go to Mexico?" she asked Mountain straight out.

"I'm not certain even he knows why," Mountain replied without revealing anything.

As if an alarm had sounded, Savannah catapulted off the couch. She marched across the wide room, turning at the door to face the others. She stood, legs straight, feet firm, the girl gone, the woman restored. "Okay, let's go."

"Where are we going now?" Cash strolled into the kitchen. He took two beers out of the refrigerator, offered one to Mountain. He popped open the other one, looked at Savannah standing coiled and ready to spring at the door. "Want a beer?"

"You shouldn't drink if you're going to drive."

He raised the can and took a long swallow. "I'm not going to drive."

Savannah patted the air with her palms as if trying to appear reasonable. "All right, all right, I'll drive. You just tell me what turns to take to get back to Denver."

Cash sank into a plump chair, propped his feet on the heavy oak coffee table. "No." He leaned his head back, tipped the can to his mouth. "I'm not going anywhere."

"What do you mean?"

"That's a rhetorical question, right?" He drank his beer.

"What about McCormick?"

"What about him?"

"The longer we wait, the harder it's going to be to find him."

Actually Cash was becoming as concerned about his brother's behavior as everyone else, but he wasn't going to take any action until he was able to reach McCormick and find out exactly what was going on.

"What happened to giving our boy 'some time, some space'?" He repeated Savannah's own cool-headed theory of only a few days ago.

She flung her arm toward the vast skyscape beyond the window. "How much more space does he need? I've wasted four days already. The wedding is only a week away." Her gaze narrowed on Cash as if assigning blame. "And your brother leaves the country."

Cash shrugged. "Doesn't sound to me like Mc-Cormick's ready to be found. Maybe all those demons haven't quite been exorcised."

"On the contrary, it's clear your brother has lost his mind. And I, for one, am not going to sit around here for happy hour while McCormick heads south of the border for God knows what reason."

She took a deep breath and prepared for Cash's retort. His lips parted, but he said nothing. She realized he was choosing his words carefully. For some reason, that scared her the most.

She planted her feet, tapped the face of her wrist-watch. "Tick-tock. Tick-tock."

"Savannah—"

It was the first time he'd called her by her proper name. This milestone did nothing to ease her distress. Her fiancé was MIA once more, and the best man had just uttered her proper name with a soft accent.

"Did he know I was coming out here?" She would stop any words of commiseration with their lilt of pity before they would come. They weren't necessary. A side trip to Mexico didn't mean the marriage was off. McCormick and she were still a couple. A wonderful couple. A fantastic couple. So many agreed. She and McCormick—the principals themselves—had seconded the fact over and over.

"Savannah—"

A second time? She braced herself as rage rushed in. She couldn't allow one syllable of doubt. Not one. "McCormick and I will be married in one week." And damn this man before her who dared to try to make her believe otherwise.

She was something, he'd give her that. She stood before him, her stance proud, fully inviting him to defy her. No one would have labeled her beautiful. Those crueler might even call her ugly, but there was a strength in those features that had made her face come unwanted into his thoughts often these past few days. A strength, an intelligence and an elegance in her bones. He saw none of her mother's pale-skinned beauty in her—only a fierceness that he knew made people look at her twice and challenged them to form an opinion.

She stood waiting.

"It'll be too late by the time we get back down the mountain. First thing in the morning, we'll drive down together to Denver. I'll get the first flight to Mexico, and you can fly back to Atlanta." His tone told her it was a reasonable offer—take it or leave it.

"I'm going with you."

"To Denver."

"To Mexico."

"Not necessary."

She pulled herself up in silent fury before him. "I'm not going back to Atlanta without McCormick."

"Mexico isn't all Cancún and frozen margaritas, you know. There's some pretty tough sections—especially for a woman whose idea of roughing it is going coach."

He realized his mistake as she straightened, taller and more resolute. He'd challenged her.

"I doubt McCormick is hanging out in the barrio. Did he happen to mention where he was going in Mexico?" she asked Mountain.

"He wasn't specific."

"It'll be easier for me to find him without excess baggage," Cash pointed out.

Her neck became longer as if she needed more breath. She folded her arms across her chest. "I'm going."

"No." His strength was equal to hers. They both knew it.

"Give me one good reason why I should trust you, Walker."

He smiled slow. "Because right now, you don't have any other choice, Slick."

"God help me if that were true." She turned toward the door. "I'm going…with or without you."

Cash took a long, satisfying sip of beer. "*Adiós, amigo.*"

"Suits me fine."

The iron will that had rarely relented since their first meeting was in the set of her spine, the tension between her shoulders. It was futile to argue, but Cash couldn't resist the fun.

"How are you planning to find your fleeing fiancé?"

Savannah's shoulders squared further as she breathed in deeply, the only hint she was clutching at her control. "I'll find him." She wrenched open the screen door. "If I have to walk all the way to Mexico."

Without a doubt, Savannah Sweetfield had made up her mind she would be married next week. The woman's stubbornness could make a man much saner than he crazy, but he had to admire her conviction.

"Watch out for the wolves," he told the woman's retreating back. He winked at Mountain.

"They better watch out for me." Savannah slammed the door and stomped off the porch to the sound of Cash's laughter.

"Woman of great spirit," Mountain echoed Cash's thoughts only moments ago.

"Woman of great pain in the butt."

Mountain drank his beer. "She makes you laugh."

Cash took a draw from his own silver can. "It's either that or I kill her."

The other man studied his friend. "It's the friction in an oyster that makes the pearl."

Cash laughed. "You know, that 'wise 'ol Injun' routine only works to romance the women guests."

His friend's gaze remained steady. "It has been a long time since you laughed so deeply—as if from the heart."

"For Christ's sake, Mountain, she's my brother's fiancée."

His friend's stare didn't waver. "So everyone says."

Cash looked past the man to the last of the sun low in the sky. Finally his gaze returned to Mountain. "What does my brother say?"

Outside an engine ignited, revved, followed by a squeal of tires.

Cash shook his head, took another sip of his beer. "Thar she blows."

"Look out, wolves," Mountain noted gravely.

SAVANNAH GRITTED her teeth as she pressed on the gas. She rarely swore, hardly ever slammed or stomped about, hated to speed and never, never in her life had she stolen anything, let alone a car. But when she'd seen the keys still dangling in the Jeep's ignition where Cash had left them, she hadn't thought twice. She didn't have time to stand around, trying to sway Cash to her point of view. The wedding was a week away. And she needed a groom—not a best man whose greatest attribute was he looked way too enticing in a "monkey suit."

Not that rescuing a wayward groom was all she had to do between now and the wedding day. A thousand other things had to be initiated, checked, confirmed. Several work projects needed to be wrapped up if she expected to go on honeymoon. She'd left instructions, tapes and lists of things that had to be done, but still, before she even left Denver tonight, she would have to call Atlanta. She'd forgotten to check on the linen napkins for the reception. She had to make certain they'd been corrected to the exact shade of blush she'd specified—not pink, not peach and goodness, certainly not orange. No sir, nothing but the color of that dusk-tinted streak in the sky that had appeared as if created for her alone. She slowed the car and saw her surroundings. The sun might have exploded, the sky an artist's hope. All was nothing but sharp rock and vivid color and flimsy, dizzying air. And great beauty, incredible beauty. Her power was nothing.

She pulled over to the road's thin shoulder. She gripped the steering wheel, yearning to have someone beside her, someone to who she could point and say, "Look there. And over there. And at that." She lowered her forehead until it rested on her knuckles and there, all alone with no one to witness or ridicule, in the midst of more beauty than should be allowed, she wept.

She cried for how long, she didn't know. Nor why. All she knew was, the more she cried, the harder the tears came. She was still sobbing when she heard a vehicle approaching in the distance behind her. She immediately straightened up, slammed the Jeep into Drive, gunned the engine and sped off down the rough road toward the sunset. She had no idea where she was or where she was going. But she did know no one had ever seen Savannah Sweetfield cry, and they weren't about to now. She wiped her tears on her sleeve.

She pressed on the gas, her jaw locking and her

face drying. McCormick and she would be married next weekend and have a wonderful life together.

All she had to do was find him.

She glanced in her rearview mirror, braking as soon as she saw the dark coupe behind her. Too late. Lights flashed.

Of course. Of course. Did you expect anything otherwise? The Jeep's windows rattled. She was becoming a stranger to herself—a shrieking, stealing, speeding stranger. She eased off the gas and steered the car to the shoulder.

"Good day, officer." She smiled big as the man came to the vehicle's opened window.

"Ma'am." She heard the twang of the West. "Driver's license and registration, please."

"Certainly." She reached beside her. Where was her purse? Back at the lodge, of course, with her other things. Cash, she thought with new fury. He'd deliberately riled her up until she was acting like a lunatic. What's worse, she'd let him get to her.

She had no choice but to smile wider at the tall, sandy-haired man. He was dressed completely in somber shades, his lined face shaded by the stiff brim of his matching hat. The last rays of sun shone on the badge on his shirt.

"This is all really just so embarrassing." She emphasized her Southern accent, having a feeling she was going to need all the help she could get. "You see, I just got into town—at least that's what they call it. I'm still debating that point. All I saw were a few scattered houses, most that could use a good coat of paint, if you know what I mean. And one well-built doorless outhouse that was pointed out to me with pride. Really. One would think there was some kind of a health ordinance or something against such a structure, don't you think? But I suppose if there was, why you'd be the first one to—"

"Driver's license and registration, ma'am."

The man's stern lines remained so. Sugaring and stalling with her colorful explanation wasn't working.

"I'm getting to that." She remembered to smile. "Like I said—"

As she spoke, she leaned across the seat toward the glove compartment, hoping to find a registration or ownership card or something. A hand clamped on her shoulder.

"Hey!" She hated being touched unexpectedly, especially by a stranger—even one in uniform. She shook the hand off, pulled away and glared back at the man with the iron mask.

"Keep your hands on the dashboard, ma'am."

"I was just going to look for the registration. You see, I don't have my license with me, but I'm sure the registration or insurance papers or something is in the glove compartment if—"

"I know the owner of this vehicle, ma'am."

She breathed a sigh of relief. "Thank goodness. So you can only imagine the type of day I've been having so far—"

"Wait here, ma'am."

"Sweetfield," Savannah leaned her head out the window and called to the policeman as he walked to his squad car. "Savannah Sweetfield. Of the Atlanta Sweetfields."

The policeman was talking into a radio. Savannah slumped against the seat, dismayed at the humiliating prospect of having to return to the lodge to get her things. She straightened, pasted on a smile as the policeman approached the window.

"As I'm sure you found out, this is really just—"

"Step out of the car, ma'am."

"What?"

"Step out of the car." He opened the door.

"Now, just a minute. Really, I can explain. Do you have identification?" Whoops. She wasn't certain turning it into a case of "You show me yours and I'll show you mine," was the correct tactic in this case, considering she had nothing to show.

"Step out, ma'am."

She weighed her options as she stared at the man's unsmiling expression. She eased out of the car. "Really, this is all a big misunderstanding. You're gonna laugh."

The officer took her elbow. "Please proceed to the squad car, ma'am."

"Whoa—wait a minute—let's regroup here." Savannah backed away from the man.

"You're in possession of a stolen vehicle, ma'am."

She gasped. She should have known. Cash was a criminal. An outlaw. Poor McCormick. Not to mention the rest of the Walker family. Hadn't he caused them enough heartache? Now this. They'll be horrified. Not to mention what others will think.

"Listen, you've got the wrong person."

"I've never heard that one before, ma'am," the officer deadpanned.

"Let me explain. I borrowed this car from Cash Walker."

"That's not the term we use around here, ma'am."

"No, you don't understand. The Jeep was at Cash Walker's lodge."

"That doesn't surprise me."

"Didn't surprise me either," Savannah agreed. Finally she was making headway.

"After all, he is the rightful owner."

"Whoa. Back up. I thought you said this Jeep was stolen?"

"That's correct."

"But you just told me this Jeep belongs to Cash Walker?"

"Yes, ma'am. He's the one who reported it stolen." The officer took her elbow and steered her toward the police car.

Anger replaced Savannah's confusion. "Well, you might as well save yourself some time and tack murder one on to the charges, too," she declared as the officer opened the car's back door, "because he's a dead man."

The officer got in the front seat. "I'd advise you to wait for your lawyer, ma'am, before you confess."

"Confess?" Savannah leaned her head back on the seat. In less than a half hour, she'd laughed hysterically and cried inconsolably. Now she wasn't sure which she should do first. Neither, she decided, calling again on the righteous indignation that had served her so well in the past. She leaned forward. "Go ahead, take me to the big house. Or do you just hang 'em from the nearest tree in these parts?"

"You're not from around here, are you, ma'am?"

"You read my rap sheet, didn't you?"

In the car's rearview mirror, Savannah saw a truck coming toward them. As it slowed, she recognized Mountain in the driver's seat, Cash beside him. The vehicle parked behind the squad car.

The officer got out, opened the back door. Savannah glared straight ahead.

Cash leaned inside the car. "Hi, honey."

She gritted her teeth.

"She give you any trouble?" He asked the officer as he smiled at Savannah. "She can be quite a wildcat. I'm surprised you didn't have to use cuffs on her."

"She's got a sassy mouth, I'll say that for her," the officer noted.

"Yeah." Cash grinned. "It's part of her charm."

She inhaled too deep, struggling for control.

"Come on out, honey," Cash invited.

She glared at him from the back seat. "Don't call me honey."

"I'll drop the charges," he coaxed.

"I'd rather rot in prison."

Cash glanced over at the officer. "She likes to play hardball."

The officer chuckled. "Most excitement Lost Ridge has had since somebody kept stealing one of Serenity's pies every time she set them out to cool."

"That's good pie," Mountain noted, standing on the other side of the opened car door.

The officer nodded in agreement. "By the time we

finally found out it was just Boomer, no one who'd ever had a taste of Serenity's pie could blame him.''

"What'd it take? About six months before he and Serenity tied the knot?''

The officer chuckled again. "Boomer swears six, Serenity says four and a half.''

As the police officer and Mountain chatted, Cash leaned in closer to Savannah. "C'mon, Slick, how far were you going to get without your American Express corporate card anyway?''

She turned a fierce gaze on him.

"I bet I can even persuade Chuck here to forget about the speeding ticket.''

"I don't need your assistance, Walker.'' She spoke through a tight jaw.

He leaned in way too close, touching her only with his intense gaze. It was more than enough. "You forget, you're talking to the master here. The original last stand. Everyone else might buy that 'I don't need anything from anybody' routine, but not me. I invented it, so I know it's a crock of nothing more than pigheaded pride.''

She stared at him, surprised at his revelation.

He sighed with disgust, whether at himself or her, she wasn't sure, and straightened. Staring after him, she slid across the seat, came out of the car.

"Your keys are in the ignition, Cash.''

"Thanks, Chuck.'' Cash shook the officer's hand. "Give my love to Louise.''

"Will do. She said just the other day she was going to be calling you boys up for an invite soon.''

"Tell her if she fries up some of that special chicken of hers, we'll be there."

"Just to give you fair warning, don't be surprised if you see her two unmarried nieces from Colorado Springs sitting at the table beside you." The officer turned to Savannah, offered his hand. "Nice to make your acquaintance, ma'am. Don't want you to remember your stay here in Lost Ridge unkindly so we'll just forget about the speeding ticket."

"That's it?"

The uniformed man smiled. "If you prefer I give you a ticket, that would be—"

"No, no." She shook the officer's hand. "Be assured my career in crime is over."

"Fair enough." He got into the coupe. "Boys. Ma'am." He touched the brim of his hat in farewell, put the car into gear and pulled away.

Mountain headed to the truck. "I'll meet you two back at the lodge."

Cash looked at Savannah. "C'mon. Mountain makes a mean Caesar salad, and I dug up a decent chardonnay that might help cool your jets."

She could feel the fire in her eyes and the beginning of an ulcer in her stomach. She strode to the Jeep, climbed up into the passenger seat, folded her arms and glared out the window. Uncertain if she should be grateful or indignant, she chose the latter, keeping her profile at a proud angle as she stared out the window, saying nothing. Not even when Cash pointed to the sky in its less dramatic stage of sunset but still as beautiful as a dream and said, "Look at that. Over there."

When they arrived at the lodge, Savannah had no choice but to follow Cash up the porch steps and into the grand room. Mountain was making a salad at the kitchen island counter. Cash walked toward the refrigerator, opened the door and took out a platter of steaks. "You eat meat, Slick?"

She stood, hands to hips. "I'm assuming you still refuse to take me down the mountain tonight?"

He said nothing. He didn't have to. His amused smile was enough.

She spun on her heel and marched toward the wall of windows. She slid back the glass door and stepped out onto the deck.

Mountain shot a look at Cash but said nothing before he returned his attention to the romaine leaves. Cash took a wooden mallet out of a drawer, slapped a steak on the butcher block square at one end of the island and pounded the beef, missing a beat only when he glanced toward the deck. The sixth time he looked up, he smashed his thumb. He slammed the mallet down.

Mountain gently tore the romaine. "It's easier to knock on a locked door than to bust it open."

Cash shifted his gaze from Savannah's stiff backside to his friend. "You're not helping at all here, you know."

A slow grin split Mountain's ageless face. Sighing more than once, Cash washed his hands, uncorked a bottle of wine and poured two generous glasses. He moved toward the deck door. Mountain didn't stop grinning.

Chapter Five

Savannah didn't turn as Cash stepped out onto the deck. It was late spring but even at the height of summer, the air was always cool and kind this far up the mountains. He crossed the deck to where Savannah stood at the rail. She took the wineglass he offered without acknowledging him. She took a long sip, staring out at the scenery, her expression as fixed as the distant peaks.

The teasing and quick comebacks left him. He sensed the sadness Savannah had tried so hard to cover with anger and action, the sadness he himself had hoped to shelter her from a little longer. That, more than anything, was why he'd refused to take her down the mountain tonight. He had wanted to give her at least one more night of delusion.

He looked in the direction of her intense gaze. "Ah, you found the twin peaks, Grays, elevation 14,270, and Torreys, elevation 14,167." He pointed. "The old Saint John's mine and mill are up there on Glacier Mountain." He angled his gaze. "And back there are Estonia, Latvia and Lithuania, three of the meanest avalanche chutes you'll ever see."

It was as he'd feared—another woman. McCormick had talked of Mexico to Mountain also. Mountain, with his wise eyes and his cryptic silences, often had become the recipient of even strangers' deepest confidences. Like others before him, McCormick had chosen him on whom to unload his burden.

Her name was Apolonia Luis. The first time McCormick had seen her she'd worn pink lipstick and a yellow dress and was knock-'em-dead beautiful. They'd met six months ago when McCormick was in Mexico scouting manufacturing sites and checking current production operations. The four-day business trip had turned into four weeks. Mountain said his brother had talked all night—of Mexican breezes, of Apolonia with a flower in her hair, the sweet thick brown soup they ate, how Apolonia would make him feel ashamed when he tried to buy her things. Finally he'd had to leave, but when he'd returned to Atlanta, McCormick could not forget the dark-eyed beauty with a crimson flower in her hair. He'd told his father he feared he'd fallen in love with another.

Without expression, Cash had listened as Mountain relayed his father's advice to McCormick—"Desire will be the death of us all." Being the good son, McCormick had complied as he'd always complied and remained faithful to his pledge to marry Savannah. Still, he was unable to stop himself from calling Apolonia, the calls becoming more frequent and his dreams of the other woman becoming feverish as the wedding drew near, until finally he'd fled, seeking distance, space, solitude to sort everything out.

Mountain had not offered any advice. He *was* wise,

after all. He'd only listened until late into the night. The next dawn McCormick had emerged sleepless and shirtless and announced to Mountain he had to go to Mexico, see the woman one more time.

"To tell her goodbye?" Cash had hoped.

"To be certain he hadn't made the wrong choice," Mountain had answered soberly.

Now Savannah stood beside Cash, striking and silent. What was he supposed to tell her? She might be the wrong choice? Did he have the right to reveal his brother's possible change of heart? Certainly that was a matter between McCormick and Savannah. What if once McCormick arrived in Mexico, he realized that what he'd believed was true love had only been a four-week fling? Shouldn't it be McCormick's choice to tell Savannah the reason for his flight?

Yet Cash's conscience argued that the woman beside him had the right to know. But was it his right to tell her, to betray his own brother?

Three days ago, he'd thought the worst scenario of being best man would be wearing peach.

Savannah took another sip of wine, her singular stare unwavering. What if she already suspected? She must have suspicions. It would explain her current uncharacteristic behavior. If so, his attempts to shelter her had only insulted her, added to her pain. Still he couldn't find the right words to console her.

"You were going west, you know. Denver is south. We might not have found you until next year's thaw."

She didn't even nod. He allowed several more minutes of silence, took in the woman's fierce profile, did not want to be the one to make it crumble. His brother had been wrong, treating this woman so carelessly.

He was about to tell her so when she slanted her gaze to him. "Did he know I was coming?"

Cash read nothing in her expression. "No."

It was the truth. Already far more involved in the matter than he was comfortable with, Cash hadn't spoken to his brother again since that last unexpected phone call. He didn't know if Savannah believed him or not, wouldn't blame her if she didn't, wondered why it mattered. He waited, sensing she wanted to ask him more, hoping she would and thus make it easier on him, he thought selfishly. He didn't like scenes, fell apart at a woman's sniffle. Yet he doubted there would be scenes or tears with Savannah. At least he hoped not. He had seen changes in her over the past twelve hours. A few cracks had opened, revealing the vulnerable woman behind the superwoman master-of-her-ultimate-fate facade. He knew she had questions. He couldn't answer them all, but if she was brave enough to ask, he would tell her what he knew. He waited.

She didn't speak again. Instead she looked to the mountains as if the answers were there. He looked to the mountains, too. She wasn't ready to ask any more questions yet. She was as afraid as he.

"Savannah—"

"I was thinking how surprised he'd be to see me." She cut in, her words quick and disjointed, as if she feared what he was about to say. She faced the mountains, spoke to them, too. "I was thinking, no, I hadn't surprised him enough, maybe not ever. I had imagined him startled, shocked even, but then, that smile of his would come, the one where his lips stay neat and tight, despite or maybe because of the degree of joy. I had envisioned a signal of pleasant delight, relief even…''

Her voice trailed off. Her profile remained firm. Only the flickering glance she gave him and the tight clench of her fingers around the glass's stem revealed her anxiety. The questions she was afraid to ask were in her eyes. He looked too long at that strong face, trying to deny its delicacy. He remembered how it felt to be betrayed by one you believed loved you. He'd thought he'd forgotten. Now he knew he'd only chosen not to remember.

He wished he had all the answers this woman sought. His brother was a fool.

She set her wineglass on the rail. Smiling, she tried to hide the questions in her eyes. ''McCormick…he seems to enjoy surprises suddenly.''

''Savannah—''

''I've decided I've gotten used to you calling me Slick.'' She couldn't completely conceal the anxiety in her tone. ''I suppose it grew on me.''

He looked at her. Why had he always thought of her as large-framed, strong, tough? She was as slight as the wind, as frail as a season and those eyes so big and brave, but with so many questions. If she hadn't been his brother's fiancée, he would have drawn her to him right now and kissed her until there was no more careful pain in her face.

And she probably would have slapped him soundly.

"They say Mexico has the most beautiful beaches." She straightened as if readying for battle. "White sand raked with as much care as a woman's hair." She smiled. "I read that somewhere."

Cash raked his fingers through his own hair. "Listen, if you believe in what you and McCormick have as much as you say you do, then go back to Atlanta, wait. He'll come home."

Only a tremble to her lower lip betrayed her.

He shook his head. "Savannah—"

She raised a scolding finger. "Slick, remember?"

He set down his glass and without thinking, put his arms around her and drew her close. He didn't care that her body stiffened, fighting him all the way. He hadn't expected otherwise. He knew all about never revealing weakness or hurt or pain. Still it was there, no matter how much denied.

He held her until her body had no choice but to relent, relax against him. Her softness surprised him, found the place where he kept his heart guarded, and with a shock, he realized it was hammering.

He rocked her gently. She smelled of the new spring air. Her head leaned on his chest as if her own heart was content. He was pleased, hoping he had given her a moment's peace, if only fleeting. He knew how dangerous and rare it was to lean on another, but sometimes, it was all that could be done.

"I'm not going to cry if that's what you're afraid of," she said.

Savannah's tears would have surprised them both.

Still he told her as he rested his chin on the top of her bowed head, "Nothing wrong with crying. Just don't get snot all over my shirt."

He felt a slight ripple in her body, heard her low, sad chuckle. She raised her head, her curved lips too close.

"For what it's worth, Slick, McCormick's being a jerk."

She batted her eyes in imitation of the Southern-belle legacy from which she'd sprung. "I do believe that's the nicest thing you've ever said to me, Walker."

He smiled at her. Despite the appealing softness in his arms, he knew, at the core, she was strong. No matter what happened, she would survive. He leaned down, intending nothing more than a light kiss, a gesture of caring to someone who needed caring at that moment. And maybe that's all it would have been if her mouth hadn't yielded so sweetly beneath his.

He felt her breath catch, felt his own heart still, then start again, the rhythm too quick and hard. He could have stepped back, denied everything with a grin and a light-hearted comment, but the moment came and changed too quickly from caring to need, from tender kisses to full passion. His heart beat again.

Did his arms tighten around her or did she press closer to him? Did he ask admittance into the warmth of her mouth or did her lips part in invitation? It didn't matter. Nothing mattered but the taste of her, the feel of her body against his.

The air was no longer cool around them. There was

only heat and a blinding desire. He buried his hand into the softness of her hair, tilting her head back, his tongue sliding inside, demanding and receiving her complete response.

Her body arched to his, fitting against him as if it belonged there, a low whimper in her throat as her fingers buried in his hair, pulled him fast to her.

She was so right in his arms. So very, very right. He devoured her mouth as if starving. And he had been; he'd been starving for years. *It had been so long*.

My God, what was he doing? He lifted his head at the same time Savannah's hands flattened to his chest. When their eyes met, he saw in hers what he already knew— *No matter how right, it could never be*.

He stepped back. Savannah's hands dropped. *What had they done?*

"I didn't mean—"

"Of course not. Neither did I." Savannah denied as quickly as he. She lifted her hand as if to put it on his but then must have thought better. It darted to her wineglass, only to knock it over. The soft sound of glass shattering against the rocks below was surprisingly sudden, swift, not unlike how he imagined a heart breaking.

"I'm sorry."

He didn't know for which she apologized—the glass, the kiss, her false belief in McCormick, perhaps all three.

"There's no need," he told her, also not revealing to what he referred. If she had imagined it was the kiss, he had not lied. Even now he wasn't able to look at her without remembering the feel of her in his arms, like a promise, taste her kiss and only yearn for more.

"Just a mistake...like before."

Now she referred to the kiss and the one that had come that morning when she'd woken him. The one he had fooled himself into thinking was forgotten as quickly as it had occurred, only now to have it reborn anew. It would take much longer to forget her honey taste, her trembling touch this time.

Only Savannah's long-honed strength kept her steady. Once more it'd come—his caress, his hungry kiss, her reaction too unsettling, too enticing, unlike any other before. Even McCormick.

Emotion—desire, fear, anger, passion—made strangers of us all, she thought. She thought of McCormick; she had to think of McCormick at this moment. How could she not forgive him when she now understood temptation, when she too had been involved in an act of betrayal—with his own brother no less. No one in this situation could cast stones.

McCormick would come to his senses, rebound as swiftly as she. She wouldn't be surprised if he was already winging his way home to her to ask forgiveness. And one week from today, the wedding would take place as planned. Mr. and Mrs. McCormick Walker—except she would keep her own name, of course.

And the passion she'd experienced in the arms of the man before her would be a memory, something to shake out and wrap around her when she was old and cold and much wiser in restraint.

"I'm famished, aren't you?" She ended the matter.

Cash was grateful to let it drop. Never one to believe passion a crime anyway, he understood how these moments happened between a man and woman. None could be predicted. Who but Eros above could foresee his brother and a Mexican beauty the week before his wedding to another? Or himself and a woman whose very denial of desire challenged him. Then there was his father's affair with a young ardent seductress whom Cash had chosen unwisely to love. He didn't accept or approve of these electric connections between a man and woman. But he did understand. These moments were life.

What he didn't understand or accept was his own reaction as he'd drunk so deeply of Savannah's sweetness. He would think no further of the shock of emotion going too deep, the sigh as if coming to the end of a long, arduous journey.

"Let's go inside." No banter came to rescue him...or her. He put his arm around her shoulders to say they would never be lovers and, Lord knows, they weren't quite buddies, but neither were they strangers. The feathery tips of her hair brushed against his arm and awareness shot through him like a panic.

He found his voice, was reassured at its normalcy even as all else around him was racing. "I'll finish making dinner. We'll eat, take our plates before the fire, and Mountain will tell us wonderful stories. Some you will even believe. I'll make you a bed where you can look out at the moon and see the sun as soon as it breaks in the morning. You'll sleep. And first thing in the morning, I'll drive you down the mountain so you can fly home to Atlanta.''

He waited for her protest but it didn't matter what arguments she offered, she wasn't going to Mexico with him. He wasn't going to deliver her deliberately to heartache, should his brother choose another. She would learn the news soon enough.

She turned her face to his. ''You don't have to go to Mexico. There's no reason.''

''No reason?'' He had been prepared for objections.

''Hunting down a wayward groom goes above and beyond the best man's duties.''

''I *am* also his brother.''

''Oh Walker, you really are nothing but a big ol' sugar lump beneath that rough-and-ready exterior, aren't you?''

She was ready to spar once again. And he did not mind at all. Already unnerved by her kiss, her uncharacteristic compliance had threatened to unbalance him completely.

''Did you know McCormick was in Mexico last year?'' She didn't allow him to answer. ''On business, of course.'' She stopped. Her face held an expression of ''Aha!''

''It would be just like McCormick to swing down there on his way home to Atlanta to check on operations. It'd give him an opportunity to save face plus a business deduction to boot.''

Now. He looked into the new light in those brown eyes. *Tell her about the other woman now.* Yet she did have a fifty-fifty chance McCormick would chose duty over desire. And anyone who knew his brother would say the odds were in Savannah's favor.

He was a coward, but he looked into that bright face and could not find the courage to dash the hope that had made Savannah's features strong again.

She was right. He'd already gone beyond his duty as best man. Whatever happened now would be between his brother and Savannah.

After supper, fortified with a good meal and Mountain's tales and Cash's banter, which she indulged herself into thinking was solely to raise her spirits, Savannah made her calls home. First work, then the family, not that the two had ever been separate in her whole life. The various members of her staff to whom she spoke assured her that all was fine. From her assistant's report, all wedding details that needed to be addressed for that day seemed to be in order. Savannah gave her a few more instructions, reminding her to check with the hotel about the linen napkins, before the erratic reception on her cell phone forced her to hang up. Cash had told her before that the mountains often play havoc with cell phones. He offered her his office phone upstairs.

She'd finished her calls there and returned downstairs for another cup of coffee. She carried her mug to the fire and curled up on the couch. Cash sat in a chair nearby, a pile of what looked like printed account records piled on his lap.

"I'm sorry. I didn't mean to kick you out of your office."

"No problem." He set the papers on the oak coffee

table that also supported his lean legs. "Person shouldn't work past five o'clock anyway."

Mountain gave a snort as he came in from the deck with a bundle of wood.

"You don't agree?" Savannah asked him.

"I agree all right." Mountain squatted before the fireplace. "Problem is getting this one not to burn the midnight oil night after night. That trip home to Atlanta was the first time he'd taken a day off in two years. And he wouldn't have even done that except he loves his brother and this is the annual two weeks reserved for maintenance and updating the facilities when we don't take on any guests and the rest of the staff takes their own vacations."

Mountain added another log to the fire. "Of course, it was Cash who restored this abandoned old building, built the cabins, brought in the extreme sports such as the annual bike race that put Lost Ridge on the map, had the town re-incorporated to keep out the ski resorts and then, really aggravated them by refusing their million-dollar offer to buy the entire operation."

"I believe Ms. Sweetfield is sufficiently impressed," Cash interrupted.

"Surprised mostly," Savannah corrected with the forthrightness he'd come to expect from her.

Mountain gave the fire a satisfied poke, then excused himself as if his job there was done.

"You should be impressed." Cash unfolded his legs off the table and reached for his paperwork. "How's tricks in Atlanta?"

"Are you deliberately changing the subject?"

"Yes."

She smiled slowly. Of course, she too would appreciate frankness. "Everyone in Atlanta is fine." It was the same bright, chipper voice so at odds with her current situation that she'd used when she spoke to her mother.

"Anyone hear from McCormick?"

She shook her head. Cash's gaze stayed long on her. The taste of him was still strong in her mouth.

He stretched his legs even longer. "You didn't mention McCormick's little jaunt to Mexico, did you?"

"I saw no reason to worry anyone in Atlanta." *Or embarrass herself unnecessarily further.* If nothing else, her reticence about McCormick's whereabouts had earned her a blatant, satisfying relief in her mother's voice.

"You don't?" He was like a dog with a bone.

"Listen, I'm not condoning or excusing McCormick's behavior. Yes, he's being inconsiderate and is obviously not thinking with a clear head, but you don't just walk away from a relationship, throw a future out the window, for no rational reason."

She thought of Cash's own abrupt departure on his wedding day seven years ago. From his flat expression, revealing nothing, she knew he thought of it, too. Now, to learn the man everyone had pegged as a worthless never-do-well was no such thing...

"So McCormick was right about you?" She sought to understand this man so much a mystery to her. "You and your brilliant business mind?"

Cash picked up his coffee mug, made of thick,

glazed clay. "Don't get your hopes up, darlin'. I'm really just a ski bum at heart."

She sipped her own coffee. "That's what you prefer everyone to think, isn't it?"

He shrugged. "People think what they want to."

"Not if they know the truth."

"People make their own truth, Slick. It's easier."

"For who? You or them?"

Only the thud of his mug on the stand suggested she had hit a raw nerve. "Both," he answered in a tone that warned her to drop the subject.

"McCormick said you were like your father. Full of the same pigheaded pride."

Cash stood, picked up his papers and his mug.

"So he was right about that, too," Savannah challenged the man ready to run.

"I am nothing like my father." *Except they both fell in love with the same woman.* "Your room is ready whenever you decide to go to bed. I'm going upstairs to my office to catch up on a few things so I'll say good-night now."

"Good night." Savannah listened to the sound of his steps on the stairs, the click of a door being closed.

Chapter Six

She said goodbye to Mountain the next morning, sensing she might hear his deep voice, his tall tales again, if only in her dreams. Cash drove her to Denver, the mist lifting as they retraced the path Savannah had come to know only yesterday. She was surprised to find she already missed the mountains, the surrounding surf of air and space that made breaths deep and thoughts enchanted.

"I hope I get the chance to come back here." She was sincere although it sounded as if she were being merely polite. "Perhaps McCormick and I will visit this winter."

"Perhaps."

Yesterday Cash's vague tone would have led her directly to doubt, but today, she found herself remarkably optimistic about "the McCormick matter." She wasn't used to losing and didn't intend to start now. She was calm and confident this morning, recovered from the emotional tailspin that had come last night, with its embarrassing hysterics culminating in that kiss with Cash. Oh, that kiss.

He returned her glance, gave her a smile. Sea level

would never hold the same charm for her again. Such a profoundly dangerous man. That kiss. One more second of sweet savoring, then she would let it go.

They walked through the airport with all its metal and hurry, the tap of Savannah's Ferragamos joining the parade. They reached the area away from the larger planes where the private jets and small carriers were parked.

"Thank you." Savannah took the bag Cash had insisted on carrying.

"No problem."

She raised her eyebrows.

He shoved his hands into his jeans pockets, looked at the plane. "Are you going to be all right?"

She waved away any concern. "If you're referring to my little form of in-flight entertainment coming out here, don't give it a second thought." Both knew that wasn't what he was referring to.

He pulled his hands from his front pockets, patted the rear ones. "You should have some tissues."

"I do." He was stalling as if he wanted to talk about more than tissues.

"Of course you do." He considered her. "Everything under control. That's you, isn't it, Slick?"

"Damn right." They easily fell into their old pattern. She set down her bag to offer Cash her hand. "Again, thank you."

Ignoring her hand, he placed his own on her shoulders and drew her to him, kissing her with carefulness today.

"You have a safe trip, darlin'." His hands dropped

from her shoulders. He tapped the tip of her nose. "Think clouds."

"Clouds, right." She struggled to remain steady and certain as the control she'd so swiftly claimed threatened to leave her. "And you, get ready to macaroni on Saturday."

"Macarena."

"Whatever." She turned away from his smile and walked toward the waiting jet, her hand raised in a final goodbye.

Cash had to run some errands, pick up some supplies while he was in Denver but he worked quickly. He was anxious to return to the peace and solitude of Lost Ridge and the lodge. The last few days had wearied him. He was making his way back up the mountains before noon.

Mountain came out onto the porch as the Jeep pulled up to the lodge.

"Your mother called," he said as he came down the steps to help Cash unpack the supplies. "She wants you to call her as soon as you get in." Mountain peered over Cash's shoulder into the back of the vehicle. "You didn't forget the Captain Crunch, did you?"

Cash slid out a large box, handed the case of cereal to Mountain. He hoisted several more boxes. The two men started toward the lodge. "I don't suppose it sounded like good news, did it?"

"That would depend on your definition of good news." The older man mounted the stairs.

"Good news at this point would be the fact my

brother is home in Atlanta ready and waiting for his bride and his wedding to take place in a week.''

''Even if he doesn't love her?''

''Is that what he said?''

Mountain set the boxes on the counter. ''It's not what men say, my friend. It's what they do.''

''CASH, THANK GOODNESS.'' His mother's elegant voice at the other end of the connection was laced with distress. I'm about at my wit's end here. Please explain to me what your brother is doing in Mexico?''

''How'd you find out?''

''He called here today, looking for you. I told him he would know where you were better than I since you both were supposedly in Colorado. I don't know who was more surprised, McCormick at the fact you and Savannah had gone to Colorado, or I when McCormick informed me he was no longer there. It wasn't even two o'clock here yet, and I almost asked Sam to bring me my daily martini.''

''McCormick *was* here,'' Cash explained, ''but he left yesterday morning. We didn't find out ourselves until we got in late yesterday.''

''Mexico, Cash? A week before his wedding, he goes to Mexico?''

Cash had no idea how much McCormick had revealed. ''What did he say? He must have given you some kind of a reason.''

His mother sighed. ''He only said he had to make sure he was making the right decision. I told him it's natural to get cold feet. He said, no, it wasn't cold feet. It was something else, something more.'' His mother paused. "Did he mean *someone* else, Cash? Is there another woman?"

He didn't know what to betray. If McCormick hadn't told his mother about the Mexican woman, it meant he hadn't made a decision yet. "Did you ask him?"

"I most certainly did. He told me not to worry."

She didn't know. "He's right. McCormick made this mess, and he needs to take care of it in his own fashion."

"There is another woman. I knew it."

"Let McCormick handle this, Mama. He's an adult."

"Who's acting like a little boy. Your brother seems to have lost sight of the fact there are other things to consider here, such as the wedding, the merger, his fiancée and her family. Poor Savannah. How's she doing? How much does she know? Let me speak to her."

"She's not here."

"She's not there either? You didn't let that child chase off after your brother to Mexico by herself, did you?"

"She was going to go down to Mexico but, well, I can't say I changed her mind. She's too stubborn for that. But something changed her mind, and she decided to give McCormick a little more benefit of the doubt that he'll make the right decision. She flew back to Atlanta this morning."

"What do you mean she flew back to Atlanta this morning?"

Maybe his mother had had Sam bring her that martini after all. "I drove her down to the airport this morning, and she got on the company jet and headed back home to Georgia."

"I just spoke to Belle Sweetfield less that an hour ago, and according to her, Savannah is still out in Colorado with you."

"Well, she's wrong."

"Belle said Savannah called her last night and said everything was fine, hunky-dory. She was just a bit jet-lagged and wanted to take an extra day to make sure everything was completely straightened out, so she was going to send the company jet back this morning and take a commercial flight out the next day…with McCormick."

"With McCormick?"

"What's going on, Cash?"

"Mama, I wish I had the answer to that question." He had a suspicion Savannah had gone to Mexico and that he'd been played by a virtuoso. No wonder she'd so willingly abandoned the idea of either of them flying down to find McCormick. She'd already decided she was going. He should have realized she wouldn't have surrendered so easily. He wasn't sure whether he was angry with her for outsmarting him, impressed by her mettle or, most of all, afraid for her vulnerable heart. It was that kiss, he decided. He'd been thrown off his mark by that mind-blowing kiss. Feminine wiles. He would've thought he'd learned by now.

"Cash, you have to go down to Mexico and straighten this out."

"What?" His mother's request brought him back from the thought of Savannah in his arms.

"You're the only one your brother will listen to at this point."

"Mama, as you and most of Atlanta are well aware, I'm not exactly a poster boy for the ol' walk-down-the-aisle routine."

"We all make mistakes, Cash. That's what makes us human. Right now, I fear your brother is in the midst of a grand one. He needs our help."

"But what if—" Cash hesitated. "What if Mc-Cormick is really in love with this other woman?"

"Is that what you think?"

Who was he to present the argument of Cupid's inexplicable aim? He himself had stopped believing in such foolishness seven years ago. Still, he did remember that when the heart takes over, the head can deny even the most obvious. In that irrational state, huge mistakes were made. He had made them. So had his father. So had many others. Cash thought of Savannah, steadfast and certain and rushing headlong into heartbreak. And he was partly to blame for trying to protect his brother…for trying to protect her.

"No." He conceded love was no more than an illusion.

"Cash, you have to go down there for me. I can't tell your father about this. It would kill him. Your father was so pleased when McCormick found such a sensible, lovely woman as Savannah."

"With such a profitable company in her inheritance."

"I know your father is not an easy man and the relationship between you and him has never been smooth. But I'm not asking you to do this for him. I'm asking you to do this for me. I've already lost one son. I'm not going to lose another.''

''You haven't lost me, Mama.''

''Oh yes I have. I sat back and just let you go. Not that I figured you'd listen to me anyway.''

''I had to go, Mama. I couldn't stay.''

''Why?''

He'd vowed seven years ago she would never know the truth. Nor would his brother. From the beginning, his father had known Cash would never deliberately destroy the family.

''I had to.''

''We all make mistakes.'' His mother sounded tired. ''Don't tell people we love them when we should. Let them walk right out of our lives because we're too proud or too scared or too angry, and then they're gone and we can't think of a single thing that would stop us from saying 'I love you,' if we only had one more chance.''

Despite all his efforts, he had caused his mother pain anyway. Still, the truth was worse.

''Angeline's death wasn't your fault, Cash.''

He realized then she'd been talking about him, not herself.

''You can't blame yourself.''

But he did. And he blamed his father.

''We all make mistakes, but if I have to walk all the way to Mexico myself to make sure your brother doesn't completely ruin his life, I will.''

The determination in his mother's voice would

have rivaled even Savannah's stubbornness. Without a doubt, his brother's fiancée had gone to Mexico.

"I'll take the next flight out, Mama."

HE ARRIVED in the dark heat of Mexico. He felt the first gentle bath of the warm, moist air and knew he had his work cut out for him. This was a place where the flesh ruled and desire reigned, either lazy or desperate, depending on the amount of tequila shots consumed per hour. But always, always desire.

Cash moved among the tourists, natives, businessmen, merchants lining the walks, holding up silver bracelets and vivid woven blankets with the same languid urge that was in the air, in the beauty everywhere around him now. McCormick had been here on business, had told Mountain he'd met the woman on the city's south side. It was there Cash went first.

The sounds of hot Latino tunes on flamenco guitars rolled out of the bars' opened doors. It was late, but the night had only just begun in Mexico. Soon the singing would begin—the song of a day spent in a too-hot sun and a night that need not end. Many nights Cash had sung also. He threaded his way through the heat and the beauty and the sounds with so much melody, wondering if he stood a chance.

He went into a bar with wide-open wooden shutters facing west all the way to the docks. He ordered tequila with lime and salt from a bartender hard-lined in the face. Placing many pesos on the bar, he asked about a woman who might come here now and then, perhaps to dance and forget about the day? He met the man's eyes. A woman as beautiful as every man's dream, named Apolonia Luis, with perhaps a gringo friend from America? The bartender wiped off the bar with a towel, picked up the bills and moved away without a word. He spoke to a man at the other end of the bar. Both men looked at Cash. He drank his shot, ignoring the stare of a woman three seats down sitting with her legs crossed high, a sandal dangling from one toe. Around him people were talking loudly above the music. He looked at that sandal dangling expectantly. He thought of his brother. He thought of Savannah.

The man at the other end of the bar slid off his stool and came toward Cash. He was short with a thick, compact strength, his face dark with the same sun-worn seriousness as the bartender.

''Apolonia Luis?'' He stayed standing as Cash signaled for two more drinks. Cash laid more money on the scarred bar, gestured to the stool beside him. The woman with the dangling sandal turned her attention elsewhere.

The bartender set the drinks before the two men. The man made like a bull did not sit.

''Sí.'' Cash's Spanish was fair. He'd spent enough lost weekends in the Baja to get by. Still he hoped the man spoke English.

The man stood on thick legs, waiting.

''She lives near here, perhaps? *La casa? La familia?''*

The man heard Cash's Southern drawl, so foreign in this foreign land. His face lost its flat expression, crinkled with good humor. He downed his drink, nodded. *''Sí.* Not so near here, but not so far.''

Cash gestured for another round. ''She is beautiful, they say.''

"Like a new flower." The man's eyes, heavy-lidded, slanted a glance at Cash. "Where the scent alone stirs a man."

"An Anglo perhaps?" Cash asked.

The man's flat face held secrets. "Many come here, taste our fruits, have their fill, go. Until a night heats and their bellies feel empty once more." The man picked up his fresh drink. "You are hungry, *señor?*"

"No."

The man swallowed the shot, set the glass on the bar with a new smile. "I have never met a man who isn't starving."

Cash tried to see past the man's face of mysteries and intrigues, but he could determine nothing. He slid his own untouched shot along with more bills toward the man. "I need to find Apolonia Luis."

The man stared at the money, did not pick up the drink. "She is in trouble?"

Cash met the man's wary eyes. "No."

The man shook his head. "Apolonia Luis is beautiful beyond reason, *sí,* but her family is with means, and their only daughter has no need to turn her back on the blessed Virgin de Guadalupe. Yet, this is a place of pleasure—"

"My brother came here yesterday to see Apolonia Luis. I need to find him."

Cash was the one studied now to determine if he told the truth. *"Familia?"*

Cash nodded.

"Dark like you?" the man asked, his fingers curling round the shot glass.

Cash sensed it was a test. "No. Blond. Fair. Slimmer build."

The man stared at Cash, made no comment.

"You've seen him, perhaps?"

"It is my job to see many things." The man still studied Cash. Cash knew that if the man had seen McCormick, now he was comparing his brother's elegant, contained attractiveness to Cash's raw, dark force and finding little resemblance. "White knights in Mexico are often not missed."

"What about a woman? American also." It was a long shot but Cash had nothing to lose in asking. "Fair-skinned, blond, tall for a woman, probably wearing high heels, walking too fast?"

The man raised his eyebrows. "So you do look for a woman?"

"I look for that woman."

The man shook his head.

Cash considered the possibility Savannah was home in Atlanta after all. Then he remembered her stubbornness. "She is looking for my brother also."

The man gave a dry chuckle. "Your brother, he is popular."

"How do I find Apolonia Luis?"

The man slid off the stool, gathering the bills and shoving them into his pocket. "She will find you, *señor,* if she wishes. Where do I tell her you are staying?"

"I haven't got a room yet."

"I know a good place not too far from here. Clean. No bugs."

It was the best news Cash had heard all day.

"Come. I go that way now. I'll show you."

Cash followed the man out the bar's door onto the street, past restaurants, shuttered shops, more bars, and small hotels with neon vacancy signs, most missing a letter or two. Tomorrow was a workday for many, but it seemed from the music and the talk and the crowds making their way down the streets, no one was ready to let the weekend go yet.

They'd gone several blocks when Cash stopped, not sure if it was the speech he heard, so distinctive from the firecracker cadence of Spanish, or if it was the sight of so much cool, ivory skin and the shock of a white-blond bob among the prevalent heavy, black dancing curls of the natives and the night's shades. Whatever it was, Savannah stood less than a half-block away, legs straight, feet planted in those ridiculous shoes, a sight not to be missed.

He stopped, taking her in, her voice full of her Southern birthright and her gestures flying wide as she spoke to a police officer. From the expression of pained patience on the man's face, Cash had the feeling he'd come just in time. *"Un momento,"* he told his guide.

The Mexican followed the direction of Cash's gaze. "Your American woman?"

"Not *my* American woman. My brother's."

"A girlfriend?"

"Worse. Fiancée."

"Aye-yi-yi. And she too knows about the other one, Apolonia Luis?"

"Not the last I knew."

"And Apolonia Luis? Does she know about this one?"

"I doubt it."

"Your brother? *El loco?*"

"He fancies himself *en el amor.*"

The Mexican chuckled. "Same thing, *señor,* same thing."

Cash smiled. He and the other man spoke the same language after all—the universal language of the male species.

"The hotel is there on the next corner, *señor.* I will take your message to Apolonia Luis *mañana,* early, before the markets open. If she wishes to meet with you, I will find you."

"Gracias."

The man looked again to Savannah in all her full-blown glory. "I leave you to the fates now, *señor. Buenas noches."* The man moved away with a smile.

Intent on communicating her distress to the officer, Savannah didn't see Cash as he made his way to her. "Not missing," she was saying, her accent more pronounced Cash realized, the angrier she got. "Not lost. Taken. Stolen. Ripped-off."

"Savannah." Cash said it so softly she whirled around, unable to stop the relief at the sight of him overwhelming her features. He did not like the pleasure that gave him.

"Harassing the local law enforcement again?"

Her relief was replaced by irritation. His comment had done its duty.

"What are you doing here?"

She made sure there was no pleasure in her voice.

Still he'd seen that relief. And she knew he'd seen it. She'd been caught, and she didn't like it. She would make sure it didn't happen again.

"Same as you, darlin'." He smiled. "We're a team, remember?"

"You know this woman, *señor?*" the officer asked.

Cash nodded, amused by the sympathy that came into the officer's eyes. "What's she done now?"

"What have I-done?" Savannah stood with the dignity distinctive to her alone. "I've done nothing. I was robbed."

"Are you all right?" She would deny otherwise, he was sure. Still his concern was sincere. He let it come into his voice to tell her he knew the real answer was no, she was far from all right. She'd never believe it, but she didn't have to be strong all the time— at least, not for him. He would not think less of her. In fact, her brief displays of vulnerability had drawn him deepest, made him see her at her strongest.

"I'm fine."

She gave him the answer he expected in the tone he'd anticipated. So he asked again, knowing the baseness that can be in man, "You're certain?"

"Why wouldn't I be fine?" Her mocking tone told him he was as close as he was going to get. "Never mind I'm supposed to be in Atlanta checking seating arrangements for the hundreds of guests coming to my wedding in less than a week, but what the heck? I'm here in sunny Mexico where, after being relieved of all my possessions by a taxicab *bandido,* I've spent the rest of the day being '*señorita*-ed' from one police desk to another. Not to mention, the consulate doesn't open until tomorrow at ten and it'll probably take two days, maybe more, to have my money wired. I have no ticket home, no cell phone, no identification, no money, no fiancé—''

She still had her fire. She would be all right. ''Please tell me he took that little box you talk to all the time as if it were your best friend?''

She sent him daggers. ''Yes, they took the micro-cassette recorder, too.''

''Let's look on the bright side, darlin'.'' Cash spread his arms as if inviting an embrace. ''You still have me.''

She was the master of the dry look. She turned back to the officer.

''As I was explaining to you—''

''You took a taxi,'' the officer recited in his own rich accent.

Savannah raised a correcting finger. ''What I thought was a taxi. It really was a four-wheeled lair with a wolf inside waiting to prey on his next victim.''

The officer's look said he had no idea what she was talking about. *''Señorita—''*

''Don't *señorita* me. I need my things found.''

''We will do our best, *señorita,*'' the officer assured. ''Mexico is a big place, and like all big places, there are good people but there are also bad people.''

''Wolves, *señor,* wolves.'' Savannah's drawl became even more indignant. ''Preying wolves.''

Cash took her elbow. ''Maybe next time you should listen to someone when they tell you to watch out for the wolves.'' He ignored her glare and spoke to the officer, "We know you and your men will do everything you can to recover Ms. Sweetfield's possessions. *Gracias.*"

Savannah jerked her arm away from his hand as he urged her forward. He clasped his arm around her shoulders and steered her down the street. She tried to twist away but he held on fast, surprised as always at her body's softness. He'd come here at his mother's request for McCormick, but, as soon as he'd seen Savannah, he realized he'd come for her, too. Nobody needed heartache. Not even uptight, neurotic, stubborn-as-sin women.

Chapter Seven

"The police aren't even going to look for my stuff, are they?" Realizing Cash wasn't going to let her go, some of the fight left Savannah. Her body relaxed as if she were tired. He probably could've removed his arm now without consequence. He didn't.

"Anything of value was sold before you filed the police report."

She sighed. If she were anyone else but Savannah Sweetfield, she would rest her head on his shoulder. He enjoyed the thought. More of her weight shifted toward him. He knew it was the best she could do.

He let his arm tighten around her, amused by his protective instincts for this warrior woman. He looked down at her jutting chin.

"I want to go home." She said it with such unexpected simple yearning, a tenderness rose inside Cash, frightening him.

"Why aren't you home, merging and surging and doing whatever all else you do in that big *high-falutin'* corner office?"

The sharp look she sent him satisfied him.

"I earned every inch of that office."

He smiled. He'd been afraid the indignation, the righteousness had begun to seep out of her. She would need every ounce over the next few days.

"Listen, I've never given up at the first sign things aren't going my way before, and I'm not about to start now. If I'd thrown in the towel every time I'd faced a few odds, I would never have been more than the unfortunate ugly-duckling sister with a token name-plate on a company door, and the punch line of every joke in the men's steam room at the company health club. I learned a long time ago, Walker, if you want something, you fight for it."

"So you came down here to Mexico to fight?"

"Yes." Her determination, her belief, sounded in one syllable. "And I don't like to lose."

"Don't know anyone who does, Slick."

Beneath his arm, her shoulders stiffened.

"I know all too well how you feel about this wedding, how you feel about any wedding for that matter, but McCormick's behavior is merely the first of many challenges I expect we will face together in the course of our marriage. Obviously, McCormick is confused, not thinking straight and unconsciously hoping someone will rescue him before—"

If he hadn't had his arm so tightly around her, Cash never would have known her shoulders sagged, the movement was that careful. Of course, she hadn't realized they were partners yet. He himself didn't know how or when it'd happened. But he'd seen her on the Mexican street in her buttoned-up blouse and wrinkle-free pants and sassy shoes that made him smile, and he'd thought, *There she is,* as if this was the way it was supposed to be.

She looked out to the hot night with its neon and music and laughter. "Did you really expect me to walk away, sit back in my *high-falutin'* office—" she mustered a self-deprecating smile "—while my whole life slips away?"

Her features fell. He was frightened once more at the response she could generate within him.

"I just want everything to be the way it was a week ago."

He had no answer for her. No matter what, things could never, ever be the same as they were a week ago. Cash knew that. He sensed Savannah did, too.

Her head swiveled to him. "What the hell are you doing here anyway?"

He looked at her in the night's neon shades, no longer certain. His arm dropped from her shoulders.

"My mother called me. She's worried. Like you, she feels McCormick's behavior is…uncharacteristic. So she asked me to come down here, use some of that 'big-brother' influence she swears by before Mc-Cormick makes a major mistake."

"Before McCormick makes a major mistake?"

Cash heard fear beneath Savannah's dry laugh.

"I'd say he's already moved into 'major' territory, don't you think?"

Of course, she didn't know about the other woman. He'd been too much of a coward to tell her. Even if McCormick had tried to reach her, her cell phone would have been turned off during the flight and then it'd been stolen. She had no idea her fiancé had come south of the border to see a Mexican woman as beautiful as her name.

"Mexico is major." He sidestepped the question as effectively as she'd posed it. He'd be damned at this point if he'd be the one to tell her. Until he talked to McCormick face-to-face and knew exactly what was going on, he wasn't saying or doing anything to complicate matters more.

She studied him while he worried she would probe further. Instead she said, "You? Your mother sent you? To advise McCormick? Hah!"

He'd had the same reaction. Still he'd traveled over three thousand miles in the last two days. He was tired and hungry and, if it weren't for him, Savannah Sweetfield would be sleeping on the street tonight. He didn't think a little appreciation would be out of order. "You doubt my powers of persuasion, Slick?"

"On the contrary, you and your powers of persuasion have obviously played a significant role in this entire situation."

What she said was partially true. He was the one who had advised McCormick that if he had any doubts, he owed it to himself and to all else involved to resolve them. Still who knew his conventional, by-the-book brother would run off to a dark-haired fantasy?

"Meaning what?" He took the defensive.

"Meaning everything was fine, everything was perfect until you blew into town last week."

"This is my fault? My fault?" He was hungry, jet-lagged, tired and had not traveled six hours to be insulted by this…this woman. "Listen, you go ahead and blame me all you want but it's your fiancé, not me, who's running around the continent. Do you think if it was up to me, I'd even be here in the middle of this mess?"

"So what are doing here?"

"I told you. My mother asked me to come."

"Hah!" Savannah released another skeptical laugh. "Since when did you ever do what your parents or for that matter anyone in authority wants?"

"And when don't you?"

Her neck became even longer, more elegant as her chin lifted. "There's no reason for you to be here." She spoke through tight lips. "I certainly didn't ask you to come. I certainly won't ask you to stay. I don't need your help."

She hadn't realized they were partners.

"No, why would you need my help? You have no cash, no credit cards, no identification, no clothes, no little reports that make your eyes all squinty and your face pucker as if you're sucking on a lemon, and no clue where McCormick might be. No, you don't need my help. All you have to do is comb the country until you find him and say, 'McCormick, angel face, did you forget? We have a wedding to attend to on Saturday.'"

"I don't call him angel face."

"And he'll say, 'I knew I was forgetting something. Thank you for reminding me, cupcake.' And *bam!* You're on the plane, sipping champagne in first class, or, in your case, spewing champagne, en route to happily ever after."

She went still as if trying to control every muscle, every emotion.

"Here." He reached for his wallet. "My credit card and my wishes for good luck."

"I don't want your money."

"What are you going to do, Slick? Sleep in the square? Well, at least, you'll have your pride. Can't strip that stubborn, bullheaded pride from Savannah Sweetfield. No sir."

Even he was surprised at the scope of his anger. Had he really expected to fly into Mexico, find McCormick, bring the lovebirds back to Atlanta where he would be regaled by one and all as the conquering hero? Since when had he coveted the knight-in-shining-armor role anyway?

She swung her head away, but not before he saw her chin quiver. He became ashamed, knowing he was more mad at a world where love didn't seem to stand a chance any more than he was at Savannah.

"Hey…" Although his hand itched to reach out to her, he knew better than to touch her.

She waved away any words he was about to offer. "I don't squint," she said. She gave a low sigh. He was a complete idiot.

He tried to apologize one more time. "I'm—"

"I saw him." She turned her face to Cash. "McCormick. I saw him."

He stared at her, taking in this new information.

"He always stays in the Crowne Plaza when he travels. It's where he stayed when he was here on business last year. He's a creature of habit, McCormick is. I know some might find that irritating but I always found it comforting.'' The neon lights reflected in her eyes hid everything.

''After you left me at the airport, I sent the jet back to Atlanta, took a commercial flight here so my family would think I was out in Colorado, cuddling with McCormick.''

''And that's important?''

''It is for me.''

She spoke firmly, but Cash heard a little girl, a little girl who had often been overshadowed or ignored, a little girl who had been no more than the ''unfortunate ugly-duckling sister.''

''I took a taxi from the airport. We were heading toward the hotel downtown when I saw a man on the street in these gosh-awful orange shorts. Bright orange shorts. They gave me a headache even from a distance. At first, I only saw those tangerine shorts, and I was thinking to myself, 'Why do some people feel a vacation is an excuse for Tacky City?' Of course, I didn't know it was McCormick. I don't think I'd ever seen him in shorts before—except of course when we played doubles once at the club with Louella and Tucker Dixon. Actually I've never seen him in a T-shirt either.'' She paused as if reflecting on this fact.

''You saw McCormick?'' Cash urged her on.

''I saw this man in loud shorts going toward the market, hopefully to buy new shorts, I remember thinking. Then he turned his head. It was McCormick. Of course, I screamed at the taxi driver to stop, thinking as I looked at those awful orange shorts, 'God, I've come just in the nick of time.' The taxi was in the center lane, the driver trying to get over, and I was yelling and he started yelling back to me in Spanish. Between you and me, I don't think it was 'Welcome to sunny Mexico.' ''

Cash heard her tumbling speech. She's grasping, he thought.

''Finally we got to the curb, I grabbed my things and jumped out, but by that time, I'd lost him. I ran into the market. How hard can it be to find a man in tangerine shorts? I looked and looked, finally spotted him. He was heading toward the street. I yelled, but he couldn't hear me above the vendors and the music. By the time I got to the street, he was getting into a car, orange shorts, skinny white legs and all. Then he was gone. Again.

''A taxi pulled over. I jumped in, told the driver, 'Follow that car.' '' She smiled a sad smile that would have broken a softer man's heart. ''I've always wanted to say that to a cab driver. It was later I remembered the tourist's tips I'd read on the flight down about the problem of thieves masquerading as legitimate taxi drivers, how one should avoid taxis on the streets, sticking to cabs from the airport, bus stations or ones you call directly. It was too late by then.

''I spent the rest of the day with the police filing a report on a taxi driver who's probably whooping it up right now in Tijuana with my credit cards.

''But here's the strangest part. Now I can't be sure, but right before I realized it was McCormick, I saw the man's head was swaying and his mouth was moving as if he was singing. I thought, 'In those shorts I would not call attention to myself with a public serenade.' Then I saw it was McCormick. McCormick singing.'' Her expression became bewildered. ''McCormick doesn't sing. Have you ever heard him sing?''

He studied her, but she looked past him, the night's lights in her eyes.

''Are you sure it was him?'' He didn't know why he offered it. Maybe he just wanted to lessen the flatness that had crept into her features.

She smiled at him, sad but grateful.

''So after you filed the police report, you went back to the hotel to find him?''

''*Sí.*''

''And?''

''He wasn't there.''

''Wasn't there?''

''Checked out that day. No record of a reservation elsewhere. Skinny white legs and orange shorts and all. Gone. Man's a regular Mexican jumping bean.''

Cash rubbed his forehead. ''Do you think he went home?''

''I don't know what I think, Walker.''

It was the first hint of doubt she'd admitted. He knew it cost her.

''I didn't want to call home collect. There'd be too many questions.''

''I can call Atlanta in the morning.''

''Tonight.''

''It's too late. If he's not there, I don't want my mother up all night worrying. Nothing can be done until the morning anyway. I'll get us a room.''

She threw him a sharp glance.

"Rooms," he corrected. "We'll get a good night's sleep and in the morning, we'll take it from there. But first, we'll have that drink you owe me and something to eat." He took her arm, already moving with long strides toward the music and noise coming from an opened door several buildings up.

"I'm not hungry."

"You don't have to eat."

"I don't want a drink either."

The woman refused to give up. "No, but I do," he told her, steering her through a throng of tourists on their way out the opened door.

There were no unoccupied tables so they took stools at the bar. Savannah folded her hands on the bar's counter as if to say a prayer, glaring at the basket of tortilla chips Cash slid toward her.

The bartender approached. "Two tequilas," Cash ordered.

"I don't want a drink," Savannah insisted.

"They're not for you."

She tossed her head. The dim lights caught in her hair, made it glimmer gold. "I've never even tasted tequila."

The bartender set the drinks down.

"Again, you fail to surprise me." Cash watched the angry gleam brighten in her eyes, her features become more unique and arresting. Without hesitating, she reached for one of the two small glasses, threw back her head, closed her eyes and downed the shot in one swallow. She slammed the glass down and opened her eyes, blinking back tears.

He chuckled as he reached for a slice of lime and

salt and made quick work of the remaining drink. "Okay, darlin', you've tasted tequila. Let's call it a big night."

She swept him with a sidelong glance. "You don't think I'm any fun, do you?"

He smiled as he slid off the stool, spying a table about to be vacated where they could sit and eat. "You're a barrel of monkeys, Slick." He gathered the money on the bar.

She swiveled on her stool to him. "Do you know I've never had a nickname before?"

He stared at her, not certain what he was supposed to say.

"Well—" she smiled "—I'm sure some of the people I work with have their own pet names for me. In fact, I read one inside one of the stalls in the employees' bathroom recently which I'm fairly certain was in reference to me."

Cash smiled in appreciation.

"And it wasn't Savannah-Banana." Savannah's laughter ended in a small hiccup. "Oops." She covered her mouth, mortified.

"You haven't eaten anything today, have you?" Cash guessed.

She ignored his concern. "*Slick, Savannah-Banana, darlin'.* I wanted to throttle you every time you called me one or the other. But you knew that."

He studied her, neither confirming nor denying.

She smiled ruefully. "How much life can a person have lived if they don't get their first nickname until they're thirty-one?"

"You're older than McCormick?"

She looked at him from the corner of her eye. "Your point being?"

"No point at all. I just assumed—"

"Don't assume anything, Walker. That's a little lesson I've learned in the past few days. I'll bet McCormick has earned a nickname by now. In fact, I've thought of a few for him myself." Her fingers curled around the bar's edge and held on tight. "Buy me another drink, Walker."

She was treading water. "I don't think—"

"That's right. Don't think. Let's not either of us think tonight." She signaled the bartender.

Cash didn't protest. Let her have her drink. She's earned it.

The bartender approached. *"Hola,"* Savannah mispronounced, sounding the silent *H*.

The man behind the counter smiled, his profession allowing him to recognize a woman wavering and to forgive her just as easily.

"Tequila," Savannah said, with the same fatal determination with which she faced everything.

The bartender glanced at Cash.

"Him, too."

"Lime and salt," Cash added, sliding onto the stool beside Savannah with resignation identical to that enjoyed by the bartender.

"So, we finally have that drink together after all," Savannah said as the shot glasses of clear deliverance arrived. She forced her smile bright.

Cash licked the curve of flesh between his forefinger and his thumb, sprinkled it with salt, held the shot glass between his first two fingers, a lime in the next two. In one smooth motion, he licked the salt off his skin, and threw back the shot and bit down hard on the lime.

Savannah watched him, impressed.

He nodded toward her drink. "Your turn."

She eyed the glass, reached for the salt shaker, stopped and looked at him. "Why are men so afraid of commitment?"

"Drink your shot, Slick."

A rare flirtation crept into her smile. "And I'll have all the answers?"

"No, you'll only think you will," he said, keeping his expression stoic. This was a dangerous game they were moving toward.

He was not surprised when she laughed softly after she licked the edge of her hand. Her gaze stayed with his as she sprinkled the salt on her skin. She laughed again as if feeling ridiculous but not really minding at all. She stuck the lime into her mouth first, and smiled at him with her wedge-filled mouth, causing him to smile. She pulled out the lime, picked up the shot. He detected a second's hesitation this time, then the glass was to her lips, and her eyes closed.

Cash watched her, need suddenly as searing as the liquor moving through his veins. She opened her eyes, her back arched and her hair swaying. She turned to him, grinning and blinking away tears. He needed to look away from this woman promised to his brother.

She pulled herself up straight, shook her head. "Woo-wee." She slammed the glass too hard on the counter. The bartender glanced her way, his expression unperturbed. She slid their empty glasses toward the edge of the bar, requesting another.

"Slick—" he cautioned.

She turned to him, eyes bright, all sadness gone from her features. He looked at her, felt the tequila in his veins, the desire in his bones.

"Hola." She pronounced the silent *H* again as she greeted the shot of tequila the bartender set in front of her.

"'Ola, señorita," the bartender, smiling, corrected her pronunciation.

"'Ola?" Savannah repeated.

"Sí."

Cash heard her first full-bellied laugh. He shrugged, reached for his drink. Who was he to preach moderation?

She clinked her glass against Cash's. "Mexican magic, no?"

The events of the past week were taking their toll.

"We'll see about that *mañana, señorita.*" Cash swallowed the shot with the sound of her laughter again sweetly, richly rising. Laughter that made desire swell. Laughter that promised it was going to be a long night, a long trip.

He dismissed any attraction as quickly as it came, blaming it on the hour, the setting, where often before a night was over and drinks were done, there would be few strangers.

The band had been on break but now returned. The music came gypsy-free and heady as the liquor. Savannah swiveled on her stool, tapping her fingers on the bar's edge, watching the others. "I wish I had a skirt like that," she said, her fingers drumming.

Cash looked over his shoulder at a woman swirling on the dance floor, the blood-crimson and black of her skirt gathered tight in her one hand as she stepped, hot with the night and liquor and yearning.

Cash looked at Savannah. "You'd never wear it."

"I know." She grinned. "Still I wish I had one."

She fell into the gentlest laughter, laughter that made him join her. Her gaze moved back to the beautiful woman on the floor. She studied her for several seconds.

"I'm beginning to understand maybe a little. Just a little…" Her attention never left the woman. "…what made him run off."

"Savannah—"

When she turned back to Cash, the laughter was gone from her face. "Slick, remember?" She turned back to the woman. "I know it's none of my business, Walker, and you don't have to tell me anything except to take a flying leap—" she faced him "—but I need to ask you one thing about that day seven years ago, your wedding day."

He'd had enough time and practice not to reveal any reaction.

She spoke so quietly he could barely hear her. "Did you leave her because you didn't love her?"

His expression unchanging, he stared back at her. "No." He told her the truth.

She leaned forward, pressed her palm to his cheek. "Thanks, Walker." She slipped off the stool. Relieved, he'd slipped off his own stool when he noticed she was heading not toward the door but toward the center of the room.

"Hey, Savannah-Banana, where you going?"

"To dance," she threw back at him over her shoulder. "If McCormick can sing, dammit, I can dance." She stepped into the circle, flush with tequila and frustration and a wish to forget.

Cash settled on the stool. He couldn't stop staring at her as if he'd forgotten she could be beautiful. She put her left hand on her hip, fisted her other hand as if gathering the curve of an imaginary boldly printed skirt and her beauty was all her own, unconscious and unaffected. Many were dancing now: *hombres* in cowboy boots and clean shirts, beers in hand; *señoritas,* old, young, fat, thin; tourists who might be teachers, bankers, mothers, fathers, accountants except for one night, this night rife with song and laughter and foreign phrases when they shared the same space, caught the same staccato beat begun by a woman in a blood-red-and-black skirt and stiletto heels, her thick black hair caught low on her neck in a heavy-looking silver barrette.

The night was still warm and humid when Savannah came off the dance floor. Sweat beaded on her forehead and her throat. She laughed for no reason at all as the bartender filled her shot glass. Again Cash was about to caution her but he heard her laughter, thought of his brother in orange shorts, singing in the strong sun. He stayed silent.

She bent like grass in the wind, leaning across Cash and smelling like something warm and real and natural as she reached for her drink. She downed the shot

like a pro and Cash knew she wasn't tasting it anymore. The trumpet and accordion blended into a slow
waltz. Savannah stood, swaying to the music sounding sad and beautiful at the same time. Cash watched
her as she watched the others, knowing, like all
women, she wanted to dance, also knowing she would
never ask. He stood, took her hand and led her onto
the dance floor. She deserved to dance.

He waited for her protest, but she said nothing,
only looked up at him with the night in her eyes. He
placed his hand on the small of her back. She rested
hers on his shoulder. He took her other hand in his.
They began to move, neither one leading. Magenta
bougainvillea hung along the wall over their heads
and the music was foreign but the harmony familiar.
His long legs lost their stiffness as he realized something he had long denied about wanting and women
and softness and music. They turned in a circle, their
bodies close and vulnerable and he thinking of all the
dreams he'd had when he was young. He knew he
would remember for a long time this one warm night
in Mexico when he'd danced with a woman named
Savannah Sweetfield in an imaginary red-and-black
skirt that she would never wear.

The song ended, and they walked back to the bar,
Cash perfectly sober. Savannah had a strange little
smile on her face. Cash credited it to the tequila and
nothing else, but she didn't seem able to get that
strange little smile off her face the rest of the night.
It was much too late when they reached the hotel, she
humming melodies of the night. Cash knew instinctively she had never drunk so much nor danced so

much nor laughed so much at nothing at all. And he thought the day had not been a total waste.

He got a room for her and one for himself a little way down the hall. He unlocked her door, handed her the key. She looked up at him, the smile still there. "You're no good for me, Walker, no good at all." She leaned against the door, eyeing him. "Thank you." She reached up on her tiptoes, brushed her lips against his cheek and slipped inside the room.

He knew it was the tequila talking. Mexican magic.

Chapter Eight

Cash waited for Savannah in the street outside the hotel the next morning. The first light of the day was long gone, but there was a feathery breeze denying the dust and humidity and sweat that would come later. Unlike a woman, Mexico was pretty in the morning.

"Señor."

Cash turned to find the man he'd met last night coming toward him. *"Buenos días,"* he greeted. "You have news for me?"

"Sí." The man smiled. Then he waited until Cash pulled out his wallet.

"I bring your message to Apolonia Luis, but she is gone. Her cousin tells me she has gone to the sea on vacation. She said, yes, the man with skin like milk came in a shiny car, then drove off like the wind when he learned Apolonia was gone. The family would not tell him where to find their only daughter. They spit in disgust if you say his name. They do not think your brother is honorable."

"So McCormick doesn't know where Apolonia is?"

"Your brother, like you, is a resourceful man, and information comes easy here for a man with resources. In the meantime, the cousin, a girl not as beautiful as Apolonia but with no less a romantic heart, calls Apolonia to tell her the fair-haired lover has returned for her. Apolonia asks the cousin to go to your brother and tell him she can be found at the Casa de Blue Bay on the Mexican Riviera, but she warns him only to come if his heart is hers. She waits until Sunday."

Savannah's description of McCormick yesterday at the marketplace painted a man headed toward the Gold Coast, not Atlanta. He rubbed his hand across his brow. The day was heating up, would be too hot soon. "How far a drive to this Blue Bay?"

"Six, seven hours. Maybe five if you cut through the mountains, but the roads are dangerous there."

"I'm used to mountain roads." As Cash asked for the name of the closest car rental, Savannah came out of the hotel and down the steps toward the street. Her chinos still had creases in them and the cap of her hair was smooth and neatly tucked under at the ends. On her feet were those funky shoes with the slim heels that didn't look healthy. Except for several wrinkles on her shirtfront and a salsa stain that handwashing hadn't removed, the woman of last night was hidden.

"Ah," the man said with a smile. "The fiancée. Good luck, *señor*."

"*Gracias,*" Cash replied. He had the feeling he'd need all fortune the fates would grant him as he watched Savannah come toward him.

"Morning, Pookey."

Two vertical frown lines appeared between her brows. She swallowed hard. The tequila had left her mouth dry and her mood raw.

"I need a new shirt," she said flatly.

"I can spare you my 1999 Rocky Mountain Oyster-Eating Champion T-shirt, if you'd like."

She gave him a withering glance before her gaze moved past him. "Who was that man?"

"I met him last night before my memorable reunion with you. He had news of McCormick."

Her gaze became alert.

"Although I'll be calling Atlanta first to make sure, apparently McCormick's questionable taste in fashion when you saw him yesterday was actually appropriate gear for a little jaunt to the Mexican Riviera."

"The Mexican Riviera?" She said it too loud for a woman with a tequila hangover. She closed her eyes, rubbed her temples. After a few seconds of ministrations, she asked in a more refined tone, "What is McCormick doing in the Mexican Riviera?"

"Actually he's headed toward a resort. La Casa de Blue Bay."

"Why?" Savannah demanded.

"That's exactly what I intend to ask him as soon as I check with Atlanta first. And if our boy isn't back up there, shaking up corporate America, then I'll rent a vehicle, stop by the market for supplies and drive to the coast."

"You're using the singular, Walker."

"Can't blame a man for trying." And for trying to deflect her questions about his brother's sudden wanderlust. Although the prognosis was getting grim, Cash was already up to his eyeballs in this mess, and he didn't want to tell Savannah about the other woman until he himself knew exactly everything going on.

"I'll have my money wired there, and there'll be a consulate office there that can issue me temporary identity so I can get back in the States. Which way is the car rental?"

Her hands to her hips, toes tapping, she waited for his answer. Cash had never seen anyone recover from a hangover faster in his life.

They rented a vehicle, then drove to the outside market, parking at the top of a steep lane. The market began at the bottom, spilling for blocks, a white church providing a calm center to the teeming bazaar. Savannah marched down the slanted street as if off to battle, leaning back to balance in her fashionably silly shoes. She had spoken little since they'd left the hotel. Still, he saw her glance more than once at her wrist before forgetting the *bandido* had taken her watch. He heard her thoughts echoed in her steps. *Tick-tock. Tick-tock.*

They moved into a sea of canvas awnings and blankets and improvised tables spread with every type of wares from radios to raw chocolate. At the food area, vendors thrust samples at them on the points of knives, causing Savannah to recoil, declaring, "Law," as she stared at them as if they were half insane. And, as if they were, many laughed crazily at her reaction, urging her, "Pick something, pick something.'' Cash bought fruit with names like colors, heavy homemade bread, cheese, chocolate bars.

Shopping finished, they had turned to make their way out of the market when Savannah spied an alley of clothing vendors. ''Shirts,'' she said, looking at the rows of stalls with a longing Cash suspected she hadn't felt in a long time. She marched toward the vendors, stepping through the wares and the jostling women half her size as gracefully and surely as the flamenco dancer she'd envied the night before.

She was sorting through an acreage of T-shirts when Cash reached her, discarding those splattered with sequins or American slang as swiftly as she picked them up. A stout woman with one milky eye watched her, her head tilted.

''Plain?'' Savannah gestured to the front of a T-shirt, then her own shirt, nondescript except for the splash of salsa. *''Nada?''*

The woman cocked her head a little more, eyed Savannah curiously.

Savannah picked up a shirt, turned its unadorned back to the women. ''*Nada.* Nothing.''

Cash translated Savannah's request.

The woman shook her head. Savannah dropped the T-shirt back onto the pile, marched off to riffle the shirts of the next vendor.

Seconds later, Cash heard a small cry of triumph. Several booths over, Savannah waved at him. In her hand was a shirt of the ugliest color Cash had ever seen.

''Don't worry.'' She held up the mustard-brown shirt completely without adornment or style of any kind. "I'm keeping track of every peso and will pay you back in full as soon as my wire arrives. It's just that, as you can see, my shirt is stained, and I need to look at least presentable when I see McCormick."

That's about all she would look, Cash thought, eyeing the shirt. He reached for his wallet when a flash of color caught his eye. He moved toward the gay colors in the next stall.

"Hey, where you going?"

Savannah followed with her heel-snapping steps. She came up behind him as he selected an ivory blouse gathered loosely at the neck and intricately embroidered along the breast.

"This one." He held out the shirt. For some reason, he wanted her to look more than presentable. Maybe so McCormick could see what a fool he'd become. Maybe so if nothing else, no matter what happened, Savannah would know it wasn't because she wasn't beautiful. He looked at the stout woman with a silver bun selling the shirts.

"How much?" he asked in Spanish.

"No, no, that's not what I was looking for. No, not at all," Savannah protested.

"You would have wanted one last night." He began to bargain with the woman.

"This shirt is fine." She still clutched the harsh yellow-brown shirt.

"That shirt is ugly." He named another price to the vendor.

"But this." Savannah ran a fingertip along the rich stitching. "I want the other one."

"But I'm buying this one." He thrust the blouse

at her. Her heels-dug-in expression formed on her face.

He shook the shirt at her. "When you see McCormick, you want to make sure he remembers why he wanted to marry you, don't you?"

She eyed the shirt. "And that's going to do it?"

"You have a better chance in this than in that shirt there, the color of cat poop."

She touched the shirt's heavy embroidery that would lie against her breasts.

"Trust me, Slick. You'll look beautiful. McCormick won't know what hit him."

He saw disbelief move into her eyes. He suspected no one—not even McCormick—had ever told her how lovely she really was with her rare, unique beauty. Like so many women, she hadn't a clue. He took the shirt, unfolded it and draped it across the proud front of her.

"Beautiful."

In the midst of the hawkers shouting and the ranchero music keening and the buyers and sellers shoulder-to-shoulder, he was aware of nothing else but her. He wanted to turn away, but it was a moment, no, two, before he did.

In Spanish, he asked the stout woman one more time, "How much?" Savannah did not protest.

He paid for the shirt and they moved on, Cash suddenly restless yet as festive as the noise and color all around him. He stopped at several more booths on their way out, buying other items for Savannah more suitable to the Mexican sun and a woman's beauty—sunglasses, a wide-brimmed hat, an inlaid silver bangle. The tap of Savannah's steps followed him. *Tick-tock. Tick-tock.* Her objections were equally intent.

Finally he finished, satisfied with the purchases that he insisted Savannah put on immediately, changing in a cloth-draped booth fashioned as a dressing room. He slipped the bangle on her arm himself. They had almost reached the steep street when a hand clasped Cash's shoulder.

"Señor?"

He turned and met an iron fist. His head snapped back as he stumbled backward into the crowd, still clutching the packages in his arms. Everything blurred.

"Hey! What do you think you're doing?" Past the ringing in his ears, he heard Savannah shriek at his assailant. His vision cleared to see a lean, hungry face in front of him, with a murderous look in dark eyes.

"It will be worse, much worse, for your brother, *señor,"* the man warned in Spanish, "if I find him with my sister." The man spat on the ground, then stalked away.

"What did he say? What did he say?"

Cash handed Savannah the purchases, ignoring her high-pitched prattle and strode toward the man walking away. He understood the other's actions…just as he knew the man would understand his actions now.

"Señor?"

The man turned. Releasing a murderous cry, Cash spun like a dancer, his foot lifting, lifting. His leg knew no gravity as he landed a kick to his assailants temple. The man's arms circled like a windmill as he went down. Sprawled on the cobblestones, he looked up at Cash, his expression dazed.

"It will be worse for you if you do find my brother," Cash threatened.

The man's head wobbled, his eyes rolled. With a thud, he fell back flat on the ground.

"What was that all about?" Savannah demanded as he took the packages from her arms and they headed again up the hill to where they had parked.

Cash waved away her concern. "Perhaps I smiled at his virgin sister last night."

"All that over a smile?"

He wasn't worried about her skepticism. He was the bad seed of the family, and he'd never had any trouble convincing anyone otherwise.

"A smile can be the start of many things." He glanced at Savannah to see if she was buying it.

"Just can't behave yourself, can you?"

Cash grinned. "Not much fun in that now, is there, darlin'?"

She blew out a breath. "Is that what they'll put on your tombstone?"

"You better be careful, Slick. I might begin to really like you."

"I thought I told you I don't scare, Walker."

They reached the rental vehicle. It was four-wheel drive, boxy and set high as a throne. He stacked the things they'd bought at the market in the back, the heat on his back, a throbbing in his head. As he closed the hatch, he saw Apolonia's brother emerging from the crowd at the bottom of the hill. Even from a distance, he could see the man's face was swollen. By tonight it would be bruised. Others walked with the man now.

"Looks like my new amigo is coming to see us off. And he's brought a party."

Savannah glanced over her shoulder, saw the cluster of men heading up the hill.

"C'mon." Cash slid into the driver's seat, opened the passenger door. "Hop in." He wasn't afraid of a brawl, although he had to admit it had been some time since he'd gotten into one, and he'd found he didn't miss it at all. But if Apolonia's brother suspected his sister had gotten word to her no-good gringo lover, Cash had no doubt the man would hightail it to the coast to protect his sister's honor. And, for once in Cash's life, he didn't want any more trouble.

Savannah slid in beside him, fastened her seat belt, stared at him pointedly until he did the same. He slammed the vehicle into gear. A shout came from one of the men on the street.

Cash glanced in the rearview mirror. The men were running now, fists upraised.

Savannah grabbed the dash. "If I get motion sickness, I'm blaming you, Walker."

He slipped on his sunglasses. "Ahh, another day in paradise."

Savannah jerked open the glove compartment, pulled out a map. "How far to the Blue Bay?"

She'd put on the sunglasses he'd bought her at the market, too. Her mirrored eyes looked at him through them. He tipped his head down to peer at her over his glasses' steel frames. "Much farther than the airport."

Behind the flat reflection of her sunglasses, he felt her leveling look. "Has anything in my behavior since you've met me suggested I would, at this point, just walk away from this situation?"

He had to admit the woman had staying power. And faith. Maybe that was the answer. Maybe her belief in his brother wouldn't be her folly but her saving grace. Maybe if he'd had more faith, hadn't been so quick to condemn seven years ago, Angeline would still be alive. He pressed on the gas and headed toward the city limits.

"So, what you're saying is 'no airport'?" He wanted to make her laugh, hear again the sweet full joy of last night.

She didn't even bother to reply, but as she bent her head to study the open map on her lap, he caught a smile. It wasn't last night, but she was becoming easier to amuse than aggravate.

He clicked on his signal and turned onto the road that wound south to the coast.

Savannah ruffled the map. "I want to take the shortest route. It doesn't have to be scenic."

Cash chuckled. "We're riding on the Mexican highway, *chica.* Gaps in the pavement big enough to swallow you whole. Animals standing in the middle of the road, looking at you as dumbly as you look at them. And for some reason no one's ever been able to explain to me, many prefer to drive around Mexico at night with their lights off. Hell, Slick, it's all scenic."

She took off her sunglasses, gave him one of those

long, controlled looks he'd come to cherish. "Are you trying to scare me again, Walker?"

"I didn't think that was possible."

"It's not." She slid on the sunglasses and returned to the map.

Soon they left the city and the Mexico Savannah had first met. En route, they learned the air conditioner didn't work, but neither wanted to lose time by going back, so they drove with all the windows open as if in invitation to the fine dust and heat. Savannah fiddled with the radio on the dash, finally found a Mexican station without any static, but all the songs seemed sad and shouldn't have been played as loudly as the wind required. She switched off the radio, leaned back, ignoring the headache that was the result of too little sleep and too much tequila. The chocolate bars Cash had bought would be soft as soup by noon.

Cash had chosen a rougher but more direct road south. The pavement was uneven, but the stench and the smoke of the concrete and canning factories at the city's outskirts was soon replaced by mango groves and lime trees stunning in their simplicity. As always, Cash drove too fast. Savannah's body pressed against the vehicle's side and her stomach fluttered as he took the curves, but she didn't scold. She merely looked forward through the dark shade of the sunglasses Cash had insisted on buying her. The bangle, totally unnecessary and so all the more beautiful, lay cool on her wrist. She was as anxious as he to get to the sea. He rounded a curve. Her body rocked toward him as if she was glad he had joined her on this journey.

She shifted, settling back in her seat. Cash massaged his forehead where the pain of the man's blow in the marketplace had lodged.

"I bet you have a heck of a headache."

"No worse than the hangover I had last time I visited Mexico."

"Been to Mexico before, have you?"

"Sure have."

From the pleasure in his voice, she sensed it had been many times. Of course, this country with its rich colors and high sun and soft sensuality would call to a man like Cash.

"Not since the fiesta in San Miguel four years ago though. Good time. Didn't sleep for two days. Last thing I remember was dancing in the square with the cardboard boxes over our heads."

"Dancing in the square with cardboard boxes on your heads?"

"At the festival's end, they shoot fireworks into the crowd—"

"Who shoots fireworks into the crowd? Criminals?"

"The church."

"The church? The church shoots the fireworks into a crowd of people? Isn't that dangerous?"

"That's why you wear the cardboard boxes on your head," he said as if it made perfect sense. "To protect you from being burned."

"Wait a minute. People stay up for two days straight. Then, at the end—"

"Near dawn," Cash detailed.

"Near dawn, they dance in the middle of the street

with cardboard boxes on their heads while the church shoots fireworks at them?''

''*Fiestas del Santo Patrono San Miguel Arcangel.* The Feast of the Patron Saint Michael Archangel.''

Savannah considered this a minute. ''But I still don't understand. Why would the church shoot fireworks into a crowd of people?''

Cash leaned toward her as if to reveal a secret. ''To fire a man's soul.''

''To fire a man's soul.'' Savannah repeated the phrase as if she had to, then fell silent again. She sat back, turned to the landscape, her cheek pressed to the seat.

''To fire a man's soul,'' she repeated once more as if she was seeking to understand. The phrase still echoed inside her a half hour later when the heat and a sudden overwhelming weariness lulled her to sleep.

Chapter Nine

Asleep, she had the contentment of a child, Cash decided, although he bet many nights she ground her teeth. But for now, her features eased, her body unfolded, the spectacular line of her legs grew even longer. The breeze and humidity had curled her hair far beyond its tidy tucked ends. Tossed by the wind and warmed by the heat, the smooth cap had sprung into life, the curls bobbing and twisting as freely as the dancers on the cantina floor last night.

She belonged to his brother.

He turned to the road and the mountains coming closer. Beneath that picture of sweet sensuality beside him lay a fierce resolve. A faith so strong, even he, who believed in little, felt its lure. He could no longer say that the possibility of Savannah walking down the aisle this Saturday couldn't come to pass. Not that she would listen to anything he said anyway. Only the birds above heard his chuckle.

Into the velvet of sleep came the velvet of laughter. Savannah stretched, lifted her face to the sun's warmth, keeping her eyes closed to the glare. When she did open them, she was surprised to see brightly colored threads across her breasts, the slim stretch of her legs exposed by the too-short shorts Cash insisted she would thank him for by the heat of midday, the dark leather weave of sandals that had formed to her foot as soon as she slipped them on as if she were a Mexican Cinderella. When they arrived at the coast, Cash had said she should buy a bikini, ignoring her protests she was more of a unitard kind of gal. And a dress with a low back and a long slit up the front. And when she saw McCormick, she should not scream or rant.

"I don't scream or rant," she had said in a most dignified way. *At least not before last week,* she'd amended.

"You will be the picture of agreeability. Yes, you will tell him, you had come with every intention of talking some sense into him until he saw what a gigantic ass he'd been. But now..." Cash's face had adopted an affable dreaminess. "Now that you see he is happy here in the sun, how can you stand in the way of a man's happiness? No, you wish him only well. Every happiness. Best of luck. Perhaps, you can meet for drinks in the evening before you catch a flight home. After all...and here you will laugh a most alluring laugh," Cash had instructed, "there's no reason you can't remain friends."

"Why in the world would I tell a complete lie like that?" she'd demanded.

"Because there you will be in your little bikini with your curls and your smiling lips and your cheeks colored by the sun and...poor McCormick." Cash had shook his head. "There you will be, right in front of him, and he can't have you."

"And that'll work?"

"Like a charm."

"How can you so sure?"

"I am a man."

"You'll have to come up with a more winning argument than that."

He'd turned, looked at her until she'd heard her own heartbeat.

"A man wants what he cannot have."

Now they sped toward the mountains, the breeze pushing Cash's hair off his brow, revealing a pagan's hard-planed profile. She didn't need to see his eyes behind his sunglasses to know they held a gleam of pure enjoyment as if his soul were here in the sun and the speed and the open spaces.

She combed her fingers through her hair, felt its mutiny. "Where are we?"

"Heading toward the hill towns."

They were making good time. They had come to one tiny town where all the streets had seemed to lead nowhere, stopping abruptly at the edge of a field or at the small yard of a hacienda and Cash swearing each time. They had circled back to the town's center, and Cash had pulled over, yelled something in Spanish to a small, brown-skinned man with a square face sitting on a bench. The man had pointed his arm toward a road snaking off the plaza. A quarter-mile later, they were back on the open road, Cash driving too fast and the breeze drying the sweat on their bodies.

"We'll be there by early afternoon?"

Cash nodded. Savannah stared out at the landscape where farm workers appeared, then were gone and candles were lit inside small roadside shrines. Hope.

The pavement got rougher, the landscape desolate. She closed her eyes, turned her mind's eye to an image of herself in white, McCormick in black, a church resplendent with music and scent and color, an image so vivid, dreamt of for so long, even now, she couldn't imagine it otherwise.

Cash braked hard, his arm shooting out across her front to prevent her from slamming into the dash.

"What the—" She stared blankly at a barricade of hundred-pound rocks painted white, proclaiming *No Paseo.*

"Crazy Mexican highway."

Savannah heard more amusement than exasperation in Cash's voice. She took off her sunglasses, squinted at the barrier. The pavement had ended.

"There must be a detour or something? Didn't you see a sign somewhere back there?"

"No." Cash drew his T-shirt off his body and over his head, wiping his face and the nape of his neck before wadding it into a ball and throwing it in the back.

Savannah turned away from so much bronzed skin, flat stomach, rippling muscles. His shoulders alone were enough to make a woman wish for unwise things. She put her sunglasses back on and focused on the rocks. "You don't just end a highway in the middle. It has to go somewhere."

Cash chuckled as he got out of the vehicle. "It does go somewhere. Here."

"This isn't somewhere." She opened her door, got out, too. "This is nowhere."

"And you've never been there in your life, have you, Slick?"

"What's that supposed to mean?" she demanded, but Cash had disappeared into a patch of scrubby trees beside the road. She reached into the back for the wide-brimmed straw hat he'd bought her at the market and walked in small circles, hoping to loosen her muscles. From behind her sunglasses, she watched Cash return, unable not to admire so much raw physical beauty. He reached into the back of the vehicle, shook out a fresh T-shirt and put it on. Only then did Savannah's muscles begin to ease.

He took out a jug of water, uncapped it and tilted it to his lips. He drank greedily, his throat working and water trickling down his chin. He finished and thrust the jug at Savannah.

"There's no cups?"

"Don't worry. I've had all my shots."

She grabbed the jug. Crinkling her nose, she gingerly lifted it to her lips and sipped.

"Well, well." Cash addressed the rocks. He looked around. Savannah did, too, but there was no sign of a detour. Only, far below, down the hill, was the village they'd just come from.

"We'll have to go back, find a different route." Cash decided. He capped the jug Savannah had returned and put it in the back.

"Hungry?" he asked.

She shook her head. He took out a piece of fruit, and took a bite. Chewing he stared at the rocks a second more. Saying nothing more, he climbed back into the four-wheel drive.

Savannah slid in beside him. He turned the vehicle around, and they headed back the way they'd just come. At the village, he followed a bus through narrow dirt streets winding into each other until they came to the Y-intersection that had first brought them into the tiny town. The bus turned southeast in the direction Cash and Savannah had just come, but then veered to the left at a fork onto a road of brownish-red dust. Cash and Savannah followed, neither saying a word, only staring ahead into the brownish-red clouds. About a mile later, the road slanted again and became the uneven but paved surface of a main road. Cash glanced at Savannah and smiled triumphantly. She gave him a small smile back, allowing him his victory. He pressed on the accelerator. She shifted in her seat.

"How much longer?"

"Just sit back, Slick. Enjoy the ride."

She shifted again, leaned her head against the seat, studied the landscape becoming rougher and rockier, but it wasn't long before she was restless. She wasn't used to sitting, just sitting. "I could drive, you know."

"That's okay."

She tipped her head, studying Cash. "Control issues," she determined.

He shot her a glance. "What?"

"You have a problem with letting a woman be in charge." She nodded, satisfied. "Control issues."

"You forget. I've driven with you."

"I'll have you know I'm an excellent driver. I've never even come close to getting a speeding ticket."

He arched his brows.

"Not before this week anyway." She brushed at the front of her blouse. "Besides, this week doesn't count."

His brows stayed high. "It doesn't?"

"No," she said firmly, ignoring the curve of his lips. "Very little falls under the category of 'typical' this week."

"So, that means it's not happening?"

"No, what it means is, when I think of my life, my real and normal life, the life I know, I will not think of this week." She folded her arms across her chest. "It will not be factored in to the total scheme of things. I'm not counting it."

He chuckled and shook his head.

"How many speeding tickets have you had?"

He closed one eye, mentally counting.

"Aha! I knew it. So who's the better driver?"

He smiled slowly. "I didn't get those speeding tickets because I'm a bad driver, darlin'. I got them because I didn't follow the rules. Just because someone follows the rules doesn't mean they're a good driver. As in your case, it just means they follow the rules."

"You get points for following the rules, Walker."

Cash's infuriating smile remained on his face, prompting her annoyance.

"Where would we be if everybody did as they pleased," she argued, "without any kind of thought or consideration to the rules? I'll tell you exactly where we'd be."

"I didn't doubt you would."

"We'd be in a complete state of chaos. Pandemonium. Bedlam. That's where we'd be."

"Or maybe just in the middle of Mexico?" Cash suggested quietly.

Her shoulders sagged. "Going God knows where…" The fierceness fell away from her voice. "In a week that doesn't count."

His emerald eyes captured hers. "It's not so bad now, is it, Slick?"

She'd never admit to him, would hardly dare to admit it to herself, but she had had some fun—dancing, hightailing it out of town with an indignant brother and his buddies right behind—

"You're smiling, Slick."

She smoothed her expression. "Where'd you learn to fight like that?" she asked, anxious to move the subject to other matters.

"Jackie Chen movies."

"Walker, isn't it lonely?" She adopted the sultry voice of a fifties film star. "Always being a mystery?"

He eyed her. When he burst out laughing, she joined him.

"See, you didn't think you could have a good time with me, did you?"

He threw her a glance but took the Fifth.

"And you know why?"

"Here it comes," he said resignedly.

"That first morning we met, you sat in my office, in my chair, and you faced a woman who has more on her mind than what time is her next manicure and how long before her D cup falls to a saggy C and right away, you thought...well, you tell me what you thought. Never mind, I know. Humorless?"

"I didn't think you had a big repertoire of dirty one-liners, no."

"Taskmaster?"

"Well, I wasn't exactly thinking whips and chains."

"A prig?"

"Admit it, Slick, you don't come off as being directly from the devil's sandbox."

"Face it, Walker, the truth is—"

"Ahh! Finally, the truth."

"The truth is," Savannah continued undeterred, "men like you feel threatened by a woman like me."

He really had a wonderful laugh, throaty, rich, warm.

"Laugh all you want, but what's the first thing you wanted to do to me?"

"My mother taught me never to say such things in front of a lady."

"The first thing you suggested I do is start dressing like one of your numerous Kewpie dolls. And do you know why?"

"Kewpie dolls? Are those the ones that have to be inflated?"

She leaned toward him, her voice earnest. "Sex, Walker."

"No, thanks."

Savannah folded her arms over her boldly-colored bosom and sat back triumphant. "Sex. That's the only way a man like you can relate to a woman."

"Hate to burst your bubble, darlin', but that's the only way any man wants to relate to a woman."

"Life's more than a roller coaster of pleasure, Walker."

"Yeah but sometimes, it can be a helluva of a ride, Slick."

Savannah folded her arms tighter across her body. "Threatened."

"What?"

"Any attempt to connect with a woman besides on a sexual level, and you feel threatened."

"No, I don't."

"Yes, you do." Savannah nodded her head. "Completely and totally threatened."

"I don't feel threatened, Slick."

"The nicknames—"

"You like the nicknames."

"Only because I refuse to be threatened by them."

"I'm not threatened, Slick." His voice took on a low warning.

"Ha!" She tossed her head. "You're threatened by the thought of even being threatened."

Tires squealed, pebbles in the road flew, and the crows in the nearby field flapped away in fright. Cash slammed on the brakes and veered to the side of the road, threw the transmission into Park. He glared at her. She glared back.

"Listen—"

It was as far as he got. She reached for him, grabbed a fistful of T-shirt, twisting it, knotting it, meeting him with a force as primitive and elemental as the land they traveled. Her hands released to clutch at his shoulders, crushing her soft, full lips to his, his mouth already open to receive her. Her teeth nipped at his lower lip. Her tongue danced and darted, lightly flickering against his until it swept inside him without restraint, full and deep.

And he lost control. It was not the first time he'd kissed her but he knew it had to be the last, the anguish and rage and need of the past seven years suddenly boiling up within him, transforming itself into one final, fierce kiss. He pinned her to the seat, his mouth never leaving hers, his tongue delving into the sweetest recesses of her tasting of honey.

A soft, pleading sound came from her as she wrapped her arms around his neck, her legs around his waist, her body responding with an intensity and hunger equal to his own. The past and future were driven from his mind, leaving only this, this one last taste. He'd never meant to touch her, he thought, as shock, desire and something more, something unwanted coursed through him. It was his last thought as he dug his hands into the thick wildness of her hair and feasted on her mouth as it moaned into his.

Her lips widened, suckling him deeper inside her. Her nails bit into his shoulders as she clung to him with a deep desperation. Her mouth opened wider, demanding, needing more. A frenzied trembling took her limbs and her nails dug deeper, clawing. She too knew this was the end. No more.

No more.

He tore his mouth from hers, dragging in great draughts of air. She went completely still beneath him. He gently unclasped her arms from around his neck, touched his lips to her heat-flooded cheek, resting his brow against hers as he struggled to bring his breaths under control. "We're breaking the rules, Slick."

For the first time, she didn't argue. He knew she didn't understand it any more than he.

He brushed a curl off her brow. "Are you okay?"

For a long moment, she looked at him, her eyes gold-flecked and opaque. Slowly she raised her fine, arched eyebrows to adopt a haughty expression. "You're squishing me."

She gave him a tiny smile, and his heart squeezed a little. He heaved a last, long breath, forcing himself away from her warmth and the fire beneath that proved far more dangerous.

She sat up straight, adjusting her blouse, pulling at the hem of her shorts. She tangled her fingers in her hair, shocked by its luxuriance. She turned her face to the sun. Everywhere was heat.

She opened her door. "I'm driving." She slid out of the vehicle before Cash could protest, but as she stood, dizziness came over her. She clutched the door and hung on, waiting for the whirling to stop. She had never been kissed like that before. She had never kissed anyone like that before, her blood too fast and thick and desire much deeper than lovely firm flesh, hard muscle, a mouth made for pleasure. She hung on, waited for the spinning to stop.

Shaky, she walked to the driver's side and climbed up into the seat. She adjusted the mirrors, fastened her seat belt, checked front, back and pulled out onto the road.

She drove in concentrated silence, the maneuvering of the steering wheel, the pressure of her foot on the gas, the feel of the vehicle's instant response to her slightest signal bringing back the control she craved. She steered into a curve, Savannah Sweetfield again.

"I understand what all that was about back there."

For the first time in a lady's presence, Cash used more than everyday, garden-variety profanity. "Listen," he told her, "it's in your 'doesn't-count' week. So it didn't happen. Let it go."

"There's a perfectly simple explanation why you keep kissing me—"

"You keep kissing me," Cash corrected.

She waved her hand. "Same difference."

"Not under the statutes in most of the forty-eight continental states."

"It's clear we're both merely acting out our unacknowledged hostility toward McCormick."

"Congratulations, Slick. Now the thrill is truly gone."

"It's only natural and healthy that I have some anger toward McCormick and his actions of late. However, since he insists on pulling up and moving on every time the whim strikes him, denying me the chance to discuss the matter calmly and maturely, which would provide me with a sense of active, positive behavior, I have no choice but to persist in expressing out my emotions in an inappropriate way. You, on the other hand—''

''Hold up, Madame Jung. You kissed me.''

''You kissed me back.''

''Okay, doesn't matter who's kissing who. Bottom line, what happened doesn't need to be analyzed for the annals of psychological study. Men and women kiss like that all the time. It's why God gave us lips.''

Savannah didn't kiss like that all the time. In fact, she'd never kissed like that, not even with her own fiancé. ''Point taken but—''

''I'm going to sleep now.''

''You can't overlook the fact you also harbor a repressed anger toward your brother.''

''I'm sleeping…and I'm not angry with my brother.''

''You must be.''

He released a long-suffering sigh. ''I hate myself for asking but why must I be angry with my brother?''

''He has what you want.'' She glanced at him, found him staring at her. ''You're awake, I see.''

''What does my brother have that I want?''

''You said it yourself. You were the oldest. You were supposed to take over the company when your father retires, right?''

''That's what my father wanted—not me.''

''Still, after college, you stepped right in.''

''Sometimes we do things not to make ourselves happy, but to make others happy. Right, Slick?''

''We're analyzing you now, Walker. You're telling me you never wanted to be in the family business?''

"I didn't want to sit behind a desk."

"But you did," she insisted.

He ran his hand through his hair, looked out at the rugged landscape. "I met Angeline. I wanted to make her happy."

"But…" She stared at him, not understanding.

"But I didn't, did I?" He finished her unspoken thought. "Watch the road, Slick."

She turned away from him to a sudden sharp curve. She glanced at the speedometer, surprised to see how fast she was going, her attention having been on Cash. She applied the brake, reducing the speed not as low as she normally would but enough that she wouldn't have to take the corner on two wheels.

"Hang on!" she called out as she came into the turn, her body pressing into the vehicle's side.

"Slick—"

She threw him a victorious glance. "Who's a bad driver, Walker?"

She turned to see a lone cow standing directly in the middle of the road, staring back at her. She jerked the steering wheel. The vehicle swerved away from the cow, headed toward a rocky embankment at the road's edge. Cash reached over to twist the wheel but there wasn't time on the narrow road. Savannah slammed on the brakes. The vehicle rose up, teetered for a second in one of those moments that always seemed unreal in retrospect. The world spun upside down. Only later did Savannah realize the scream she heard was hers.

Chapter Ten

The vehicle landed on its top, hitting with a force that made Savannah's teeth crack against each other. Up was down. Her legs were tucked into her chest, her head meeting her knees.

"Are you all right?"

She heard the thick concern in Cash's voice. She had not wanted to cry until then.

"I've had better days, Walker."

She heard his chuckle. The urge to cry dissolved. She tried to lift her head against its metal pillow.

"Don't move."

She felt him before she saw him, his hands coming alongside her to trace her collarbone, the length of her neck. From the corner of her eye, he came partially into view.

"Good thing this four-wheeler is built like a steel tank or we'd be in real trouble now."

"As opposed to what?" She saw a gash split his forehead.

"You're bleeding."

"But I'll bet I'm still pretty." He dismissed her alarm.

His fingers splayed around her throat, found the knob of her spine, worked their way gently down, then back up. "Anything? Any pain?"

"I'm just bruised, is all. You're the one bleeding."

"Just a scratch. Move your head side to side. Carefully."

She did as she was told.

"Arms? Legs?"

She moved each in the space permitted. Convinced, he said, "I'm going to crawl out the back, see if the rear hatch will open."

She watched him shimmy toward the back. The heat closed in, the sweat trickling down her spine, prickling behind her knees. She unbuckled her seat belt. Finally the door beside her wrenched open. She leaned the opposite way to keep from tumbling out. Cash was revealed in the sun's strong glare painting him a magnificent figure. She squinted up at him. Her new sunglasses were gone.

"I'll bet you never had an accident until this week either?" But his smile was gentle.

"Get me out of here."

He reached in and slid his arms under her armpits, turning her carefully to pull her out of the vehicle.

Savannah unfolded her legs and stood, her body seeming slack. She wanted to lean against Cash's strength behind her. She straightened, forcing her legs solid.

"Easy now." Cash guided her to the vehicle, made her sit against its side. "Let's make sure you're all right."

Savannah stared at the cut on his forehead where

the blood was beginning to dry and tried not to think about his hands on her body.

He sat back on his haunches. "Everything seems in working order."

Self-conscious beneath his gaze, she started to push herself up. He placed a restraining hand on her forearm.

"Sit a few more minutes. You've had quite a ride."

She glanced at his cut. "I bet I look better than you."

He laughed as he stood. He walked to the opened hatch, reached inside and pulled out a T-shirt and the jug of water. He wet the cloth, dabbed at his forehead.

"Let me help you with that." Savannah rose before he could protest. "Sit." She took the wet cloth from him, knelt down. "That'll teach you to wear your seat belt."

They were too close, his heat rivaling the Mexican sun. She rose, stood, feeling dizzy, blaming it on the sudden movement. She reached behind her for the solidness of the vehicle.

"Sit down, Slick." He eased her again to the ground, her back propped against the vehicle. "You've had quite a jolt."

She watched the cow sauntering back from whatever field it'd gotten away from. "What do we do now?"

He shrugged. "We passed a village not too far back. We can wait here for someone to come along and give us a ride or we can start walking. I'll have to file a report, call the car rental's main office, arrange for a tow. I imagine renting another vehicle will be difficult considering the circumstances. We'll have to hire a driver to take us the rest of the way.''

"Let's get going then.'' She accepted the hand he offered and stood. They started toward the village, the sun high in the sky, and the new leather of Savannah's hurraches firm on her feet.

They walked, silent, listening for the sound of an approaching engine. Clusters of black birds above wheeled and swerved toward the horizon. The sun shimmered in waves around them as if they were no more than a hallucination.

"A week ago,'' Savannah broke the silence. Her feet kicked up clouds of dust as she walked. They were a long way from the village.

"A week ago. Seven days from today. I was a competent, respected top executive at Sweetfield Corp. about to marry a wonderful man in a one-of-a-kind wedding, which was coming together like clockwork, I have to say. Seven days ago. And everything as perfect as perfect could be.''

She took off the straw hat she'd retrieved from the hatch to wipe her brow on her sleeve. Cash carried the rawhide duffel with the jug of water, some fruit, the few clothes he'd brought. Savannah hadn't bothered with the one outfit she'd worn on the flight down. She had nothing at this moment but the clothes she wore.

She combed her fingers through her hair. The curls seemed to only multiply around her face, wild and wanton. "Since that day when I awoke, everything as perfect as perfect could be, I've almost been arrested for possession of a stolen vehicle, robbed by a bandido on four wheels, gotten drunk on tequila, actually asked someone to call me 'Slick,' almost been killed by a cow, and my fiancé has run off in the middle of the night to the Mexican coast. Five days from a wedding most of Dixie's social register plus a good portion of Wall Street has been waiting for, here I am, in the middle of nowhere, walking to only the good Lord above knows where with nothing more than the clothes on my back and a man who dances at dawn with a cardboard box on his head. And…'' She ended with a crescendo. "…I'm sweating.''

She faced Cash. "What happened, Walker?''

He smiled not unkindly, wrapped an arm companionably around her shoulders and gave her a squeeze. She was too much at a loss even to stiffen her shoulders.

"Life, Slick. That's all. It doesn't always follow the rules.''

She wasn't defeated enough not to throw him a scathing look.

"Just when you think you have it all figured out, it throws you a whammy and the fun begins all over again.''

She sighed, as if she wished she could allow herself to drop her head on his shoulder. "I'm not having fun, Walker.''

"Ready to go back to Atlanta?''

She pulled up short, her expression earnest. "You know, McCormick and me, I'm not saying it was ever love at first sight or any of that Hollywood, fairy-tale, one-day-your-prince-will-come hooey-balooey. Any self-actualized woman of this century knows you don't just look at someone and fall in love forever and ever.'' She put her hands to her hips.

"But we were a good team, Walker.'' Her voice returned stronger. "And one day, we'd be great. Maybe it wasn't magic, but it was something.''

"You don't have to explain anything to me, Slick.''

"It was something real and solid,'' she continued as if she had to say it aloud. "There was mutual respect and admiration and shared goals. We did laugh, you know. Oh sometimes, you should have heard us laugh.''

She realized that all this time she had been speaking in the past tense. She spun and started once more toward the village, her steps strong and swift, even though the leather straps had begun to cut into her feet's swelling flesh. "C'mon, Walker, we've got five days to find your brother, knock some sense into him and get back to Atlanta. We've got a wedding to attend on Saturday.'' She didn't look back.

Beneath the sharp blue sky, Cash watched her, enjoying the snap of her well-shaped rear end and fearing that neither his brother nor any man stood a chance.

THEY CAME into town on the back of a chicken truck, Savannah's bare legs dangling from the lowered gate and feathers floating all around. The truck curved left, right, as it headed toward the green hills, the stacked wire cages rattling until the village of whitewashed buildings and red roofs was revealed.

The truck slowed and idled at the village's edge for

them to hop off. *"Gracias, gracias,"* Savannah called, truly grateful to the dark-skinned driver who showed tiny, pointed teeth when he smiled. She waved, smiling wide for the gift of a ride in a chicken truck and wondered whether, like her fiancé, she too had gone a little crazy.

Stray dogs came up to greet them, kicking up dust. They headed into the village, the laundry waving welcome across the flat terra-cotta roofs; barefoot children followed Cash as if he were a Pied Piper of pesos. She would wait in the square while Cash called the rental agency, filed an accident report. She moved around a bright green sign with guavas, melons and bananas on it that said Las Fruta stuck smack-dab in the middle of the street, stopped to look in a shop window, saw her own shimmering reflection. Her arms had browned and freckled. The blouse, no matter how many times she tugged it up, insisted on falling off one shoulder or the other. The sensitive stretch of flesh along the blouse's low-curved neckline had reddened. Red and brown, no more than the dust the dogs kicked. The breeze on the ride here had stolen her straw hat, leaving her head bare. Her hair was no longer her own but a dervish's dream, and the sunglasses so quickly lost had left white rings of pale, protected flesh around her eyes so she looked continually surprised. Surprised she was to be chasing across the continent after a man who'd run off with no explanation little more than a week before they were to marry. A chicken feather flew from her hair. She laughed from her soul, causing even the shy glances of the women walking past to linger. *El loco.*

She walked past a pink church. A woman with a bucket of calla lilies on her head crossed the small, thronged plaza. Farther on, Savannah saw the rise of a hotel crowned by an impossible white dome, cooled by coconut palms and hand-painted tile. She sat down on a wrought-iron bench, sweaty and dusty in strange clothes in a strange land, hungry, hot and without resources, so very far from home.

Much later, Cash came to where she waited. "A tow's being sent up. The papers have all been filled out. We can hire a driver at the hotel." He indicated the building that had caught Savannah's attention.

Savannah gazed at the building that might have rivaled the Taj Mahal. "I have a big bath back home. A big, oval bath with black-and-white marble all around it."

"Very stylish." Cash sat down beside her as if tired, too.

"You betcha," Savannah seconded. "With brass trim and brass fixtures that make every cleaner I have mutter under their breath."

"I believe that."

"Once I came home a day early from a business trip, heard the water running, assumed my cleaning woman was upstairs, swearing at the tub. But when I went up, I found her in the tub. All the jets were a-going, and she was up to her earlobes in the French bubble bath Mama brings us back from the Paris shows each spring. It was the middle of the day, the sun was streaming in, but the woman had lit all the candles around the tub's edge and the bathroom smelled like how I'd always hoped Heaven would smell. The woman was singing, 'That Man of Mine.''' Savannah smiled. "She had a terrible voice."

Cash waited, but when Savannah said nothing more, he had to know. "What'd you do?"

Savannah looked at him as if she'd been some-where else. "Oh, I left before she saw me. Went to the office, worked for about four hours until I was sure she was gone. Then I went home." She shrugged. "I figured somebody might as well make use of that tub."

She made her face stern, but only said, "I'll bet that woman's splashing around right now."

She was watching a woman with a long black braid stopped on the cobbled street when she felt Cash's fingers on her arm in a gentle touch that made her want to smile and cry at the same time. She couldn't decide if he consciously knew the power of tender-ness or if the caress, so light a woman rose to meet it, was instinct. If the former, he was a risky man; if the latter, he was a lucky man. Either way, this kind of attendance could make a woman crazy in her heart. And whether instinctive or carefully schooled, Cash possessed that power. His fiancée must have wept openly when he left her.

She stood abruptly, looked down at the self she barely recognized, brushing the dust off her thighs. "Ready?"

He rose slowly. "Thanks."

She brushed off the seat of her pants, the palms of her hands. "For what?"

"For not giving up on my brother."

She started off. "Don't patronize me, Walker."

He smiled as if satisfied as they fell into step beside each other. "You can't take a compliment, can you?"

"That was a compliment? That's the best the infamous Cash Walker, world-renowned ravisher of women's hearts, can do?"

"Keep flattering me like that, and I may have to kiss you again."

The idea was much too appealing. Savannah's steps became quicker, although she wasn't even sure where they were going. "Are we going to hire a driver or not?"

Cash pointed toward the distant palace. "First we'll eat lunch."

She fussed all the way, pulling at her lovely curls she seemed to hate so, lamenting the loss of her clothes, the newly-freckled skin of her arms. He watched her now from the hotel's lobby as he made his calls to his mother and Colorado. She sat in a large curved-back chair on the hotel patio, admiring the groomed gardens, and he knew what she did not. That she, with her long fingers and longer legs and sturdy steps and the fierce belief which would be her salvation or her ruin, was beautiful. The heat and anger and emotion and undercurrent of sex and sorrow that was Mexico had done their magic. Her shoes with the dangerous heels and too-thin straps were gone, replaced by those she probably thought ugly but that gave her a peasant's sturdy footing and slowed her steps so that her hips swayed wide in a wonderful rhythm. Her lips were reddened by guava, her eyes bright with Mexican beer and the curls that kept coming caught the light as if vying with the embroidered colors that ran across her high, proud breasts.

A waiter, elegantly dressed even in this heat in a double-breasted jacket, brought her a platter of *churros*.

The waiter smiled down at Savannah. "So many newlyweds go to the beaches, but those who know Mexico come to the silver cities."

His English was flawless as though he'd practiced often. Savannah shook her head, felt her curls dance. "No, no, we're not newlyweds. Not even close."

The young man with the eyes that would cause many women to fall in love with him took a deep breath in, his eyes heavy-lidded, as if savoring the sound of Savannah's voice. Cash had teased her that the waiter was so charmed by her accent, he was finding excuses to make her talk her rich, fluid speech.

"Soon," the waiter said, adopting an expression of wisdom that belied his age.

Savannah shook her curls, laughing outright now.

"*Sí.*" The waiter's dark eyes were earnest. "I see him, the *señor*, watching you." He waved his hand in the direction Cash had gone to make calls. "You do not have to worry. He looks at you like a lover."

Savannah stopped laughing. Of course, the waiter was fluent in the ways of charm and small talk aimed to flatter each patron's need. But his skills were not serving him today. He would be wise not to make any bets at the dog races this evening.

Cash returned, sat across from her in the exotic fan-backed chair, and reached for the pastry, his fingers dusted with brown sugar and cinnamon.

"Did you reach your mother?" Savannah asked. She had checked in with her own mother and her assistant as soon as they'd arrived at the hotel. Both Belle and her staff were frantic when they learned she would be away another day. She'd assured them she'd be back tomorrow. "Will you?" Cash had asked when she'd relayed the conversation. She'd nodded her head. She had no time for doubt.

"Yes, I reached her," Cash answered Savannah's question. "No word from McCormick."

Savannah didn't know whether she should hope or despair at this news. "Anything else?"

Cash chose his words carefully, trying to decide which would soften, which would slice. Cash's mother had told him Belle Sweetfield was doing her best but the engaged couple's absence had become conspicuous. The whispers had risen to overt rumors. Meanwhile, Savannah's father had taken to suspecting that McCormick and his family had conspired to make fools of them all.

"Well…"

Savannah pushed back the reed chair and stood as if his hesitation was enough to tell her everything she needed to know. "It's not far, is it? The Riviera?"

He looked at this woman with little else at the moment but the clothes on her back and a cynical, almost-stranger for a partner. It didn't matter that his brother was here in this land of mystery and heat with a dark-eyed dream. Nor did it matter that back in Georgia mothers were frantic, fathers furious, and half of Atlanta was making bets as excuse after excuse was offered as to why the bride-to-be was no longer available to harass about coaster engravings and the correct chill of champagne scheduled to be consumed like elixir from the river of youth five days from now.

None of that mattered because here was this woman before him, right now, ready to say without hesitation to a blatant skeptic such as himself, "It's not far, is it?'' She still believed. A Southern belle with the same streak of divine righteousness that had fired up her Civil War ancestors who refused to surrender.

He wanted her to win, he realized. Had wanted her to win all along. Two separate individuals, as apart as apart could be, brought together through a power not much more than a mystery. Maybe, for no other reason than he wanted to believe again it could happen.

She was waiting for his answer, her fruit-stained lips pursed, her leather shoes slapping the cobblestones.

"It's closer than before," he answered her, resisting the urge to kiss her once more.

THE VAN needed a new muffler, and the driver drove furiously as if he sensed the young woman's urgency although Savannah knew he didn't. Many here drove in this style, with the screeching of brakes and the shouts in Spanish. Still, she liked to think the whole world had joined her on this pilgrimage. Over the past several days, her sense of self, her very reality, had been altered. If she lost now, she feared all else would follow. So, it was understandable she choose to believe the driver in front of her now, with his silver belt buckle and baseball cap, slowing down only for the deep dirt holes in the thin asphalt, had joined her journey.

They reached the resort. The road became smoothly paved and shaded with coconut palms; the houses, against which the lowering sun still glinted, bright and white. The gardens were lush with lavender and fuchsia, and even a dog Savannah spied behind an iron gate was fat and long-haired.

The van pulled into the courtyard of a hotel, mother of pearl and so high, Savannah had to drop her head back to take in its full tower.

"La Casa de Blue Bay," the driver announced. "The finest accommodations on the Pacific Gold Coast."

The hotel doorman stepped forward and opened the door and Savannah slid out. As Cash paid the driver, she looked around at the tourists, some brown, others only burnt, milling in the golden light, at the white, combed beach beyond.

Her steps were strong and steady until she got to the hotel's entrance. The doorman pulled back the door, smiling at the couple. Savannah stopped.

Cash took her elbow. He was here, too, she remembered. She'd never let on, but she was grateful.

"Ready?" He tipped his head toward the lobby, his hair too long, deliberately defiant.

"I was born ready," she answered with a false bravado she knew he saw right through.

He steered her through the high front doors. As they moved toward the paneled desk, Cash had the strong urge to take Savannah's small hand in his. She would become angry with him, he knew, but he sensed she would have held on, becoming even angrier at herself.

"Buenos noches, señora, señor." The front-desk clerk greeted them—one more couple on holiday.

"Hola," Savannah said—correctly.

"Checking in?"

"Actually we need to know what room McCormick Walker is staying in?"

"Señor Walker?" The clerk hit several buttons on the computer. He looked placidly back up at Savannah. "No."

"No?"

Cash was certain Savannah rued her startlingly loud voice. He was proven correct when she spoke again in a hushed manner.

"Pardonnez-moi, señor," she mixed her foreign languages, causing the clerk to consider her queerly, "what do you mean *no?*"

The man, well-advised of American ways and remembering there would be tequila tonight at the end of the shift, restored his polite expression. "La Casa de Blue Bay has no Señor Walker listed."

"That's impossible. We were told he was here. Check again." Savannah's voice stayed normal, but her tone was firm. "Check again." The unnecessary repetition of the request betrayed her anxiety.

"Please," she added. "We've come a long way." She might have been in Oz speaking to the Wizard.

The man scrolled down the computer's screen once more.

"I'm sorry."

"Check again." Savannah's controlled tone was thinning.

"Slick—"

She swung her head and looked up at him desperately as if that silly nickname would save her. He didn't care if she got angry. He took her hand. He turned to the man behind the tiled counter. "Perhaps he *was* here?"

A man who has lived his life in service and one step away from the barrio has learned long ago to indulge those from *el norte*. The clerk dropped his gaze to the computer screen once more.

A smaller man with crisp steps came out a door behind the desk, glanced at the employee, smiled at the Americans. "Welcome to La Casa de Blue Bay. Is there a problem?"

The clerk spoke in rapid Spanish while the other man nodded, smiling at Savannah and Cash. He checked the computer screen.

"Are you certain your friend Señor Walker came here to La Casa?"

"We were told he was here at this hotel."

"I'm sorry. Perhaps he chose another hotel?"

Savannah looked down, realizing she was clutching Cash's hand. She jerked it away, spun on her heel and marched away from the desk.

"Gracias." Cash told the men and went to Savannah, who was standing in the center of the lobby, hands on hips, toe tapping, two even lines furrowed between her brows.

"Where is he?" she demanded.

"Listen, I'll see if we can get a couple of rooms here. Then we'll start checking the other hotels."

Savannah plopped into a chair, agreed with a disheartened wave of her hand. Cash headed back to the front desk. Savannah stared unseeing at a high splay of flowers center court and did not understand the one overwhelming emotion that had not yet released her.

Relief?

It had come, spreading like a scourge when she'd heard that McCormick wasn't here. She should be disappointed, furious, frustrated that McCormick was still missing and that this ordeal had not yet come to a satisfactory conclusion.

But relief?

Those damn kisses, she thought. And Mexico and the heat and her fiancé running off the week before their wedding. And a thousand other little details that added up to one unbelievable truth.

She was attracted to Cash. And she wanted him in a most unladylike way.

She was a bigger fool than even she'd imagined.

She pressed her knees together, folded her hands in her lap and told herself to review the situation. As she had realized herself, her feelings for Cash were no more than displaced anger at McCormick's betrayal that she had not yet had a chance to express. Except in passionate, toe-curling kisses with the best man.

The desk clerk handed Cash back his credit card along with the room keys.

"Could I ask one more favor, *por favor?*" Cash said before he returned to Savannah.

"Certainly, *señor.*"

"Could you look to see if there is a room registered under the name Apolonia Luis?"

Chapter Eleven

"*Sí,* Señorita Luis is a guest here. Room 502. You can dial her directly from your room."

The woman was here. McCormick could still be here. If not, Apolonia might have heard from him and know where he was. Savannah was sitting stiffly in a lobby chair beside a potted palm. Suppose McCormick and the woman came in, walked across the lobby, laughing, holding hands. Cash didn't want Savannah to find out like that. He had to find McCormick.

"C'mon, Slick." He waved the room keys. "We'll freshen up and go out on the town."

She stood. "I want to start calling the other hotels. Find McCormick…if he's even here." Frustration tightened the muscles around her mouth. "I'll just have something sent up from room service."

"Room service?" He took her arm and turned her to the view past the open end of the lobby. "Look. Look where you are, and you're going to sit in your hotel room? No. We'll go out to dinner, then come back and start calling the other hotels."

He steered her to the elevators as he spoke. Passing

a full-length, tiled mirror, she saw herself—tight denim and embroidered breasts and coarse hair, a wide turquoise bangle at her wrist and no expression.

"I'm not going out like this." Defeat had crept into her tone.

"Of course not." He pulled her toward the row of shops branching off from the lobby. "It's time to buy that dress we talked about. And silly shoes like the ones you like to prance around in."

"I don't prance."

"And silver earrings that dangle to your shoulders and—"

"Stop. No."

He ignored her protests. "And when you see McCormick, he will realize what a fool he's been."

She pulled her arm away from his grasp. "We don't even know if McCormick is here."

He faced her. "No, we don't know if McCormick's here but if he is, I'll bet the farm he's not in his room, ordering room service. Besides I'm on the Mexican Riviera and I'm going out and I want to share the evening with a beautiful woman."

"There are many beautiful women here. I'm sure you'd have no trouble convincing one to accompany you."

"I want *you*, Savannah."

His voice alone set off a wave of awareness through her. Even if she had been able to deny him, she sensed she would have been the first woman to do so.

So she shopped, letting Cash help her select clothes and accessories she would have never considered before. Then again, there were many things Savannah would have never considered before this week.

He carried her packages into her room, set them on the wide bed and left for his own room across the hall, two doors down. He locked the door and called Room 502, but there was no answer. He left a message and his room number, hoping Apolonia would call before he went out for the evening. He showered, dressed in the new shirt and pants he had bought for himself while Savannah had been fussing over dresses. An hour later, he rang Apolonia's room once more, left another message when there was still no answer. He'd have to try again when he got back later. He only hoped, if McCormick was here, that his and Savannah's paths didn't cross—at least not until he had a chance to talk to his brother and find out exactly what was going on. He went down the hall to Savannah's room.

Savannah heard the knock, checked her reflection one more time before answering the door. She straightened the bodice of her dress, wondering what it was like to have cleavage. Hair spray had helped tame some of her more unruly curls into a state of soft bounce. At least the sun-reddened skin along her bony chest and shoulders had turned to a warm brown. There was another rap. She shrugged at her reflection. It'd have to do.

She opened the door to find Cash, handsome and strong, the light color of his shirt emphasizing the tan that had deepened even further beneath the Mexican sun. She recognized admiration in his eyes as he took in the dress's rich tones, the full skirt not unlike the one she'd envied only last night. He brought his gaze to her face and smiled, the smile she had feared from the very start. A hush held her heart as if this were a real date and he her lover.

"McCormick will get down on his knees and beg your forgiveness."

Perhaps, she thought as she picked up the small purse containing only her room key and the ruby lipstick she'd bought earlier, but as she let the door close behind her, it was Cash she went to.

"We could stop at any hotels we pass and check if McCormick's registered," she suggested, trying not to notice the lovely feel of his arm around her shoulders.

"Much easier to call when we return." Cash pushed the elevator button.

"But—"

"Are you dancing tonight?" He interrupted before she could even begin her argument. "Salsa, cha-cha, rumba, tango?"

"I danced enough last night, thank you."

"You can never dance enough, Slick."

They moved out onto the street, into the evening. "Last night, I wasn't myself. It'd been a long day, I was frustrated and tired—"

"You didn't commit a federal crime. You had a few drinks, a few dances. Some fun."

"I'm not here to have fun, Walker."

"But you had some, didn't you?"

She was finding it increasingly difficult not to return his wicked smile. Okay, she'd had fun, a grand time actually. In fact, the first fun she'd had in a long time.

"There's a time and a place for fun."

"And no." Cash gestured to the soft night, the beach, the sounds of laughter and music calling all around them. "It would not be here, would it?"

She realized she loved the sound of his laughter.

They went into a restaurant with salsa music coming from the front. They sat on the patio looking out to the sea, and ate strips of marinated chicken and beef rolled in tortillas. When a woman came by selling flowers, Cash insisted Savannah have one. He leaned over to tuck the flower behind her ear himself, then sat back with a thoughtful expression on his face, and she, cheeks flushing, felt silly and sexy at the same time.

"So…" Cash's expression turned uncharacteristically sober. "Have you thought what you are going to do when we finally catch up with that rascal brother of mine?"

Savannah swirled cream into her cinnamon-laced coffee. "What do you mean?"

"Do you have a plan?"

"I always have a plan."

"I didn't doubt that for a second."

"First order of business is to find him." She spooned too much sugar into her coffee. "Which is proving a little more difficult than anticipated."

"But once you do find him, what will be the course? Are you going to take my advice and not stage the ugly scene he is probably preparing for right now?"

"I'm weighing your suggestion against other alternatives."

"You aren't going to fall to your knees and beg him to marry you, are you?"

She met his grin. "Never."

"I didn't think so. So what are you going to do? Talk to him in your rational, reasonable manner? Remind him of all your plans, your goals and ends and means? Things to do and successes to succeed?"

"Seems like a practical approach."

"Oh boy."

"Oh boy?"

Cash leaned toward her again, and she cursed her flaming cheeks. "Once more, look around you, darlin'."

She rolled her eyes, but did as he asked.

"What do you see?"

"Tables, people, food," Savannah recited.

"Lights, water, colors," Cash continued. "Everywhere pleasure and beauty. You can feel it in the heat on your skin, sense it in the air like a lover's arms. This is where McCormick came. He ran here."

Her gaze veered back to him.

"Now you chase after him, find him, and what's the temptations you use to lure him home, into your arms for eternity?"

The gold in her eyes darkened.

"Responsibilities. Obligations. Commitments. Long days, hard nights. Companies merging. Fortunes building. Work, work and more work."

"That's not all there is," Savannah argued.

"Doesn't sound like much fun to me, Slick."

"As I said before, there's a time and place for fun."

Cash gestured to their surroundings. "I'm not saying you're right or I'm wrong. All I'm saying is McCormick came here. This is where he ran."

She pressed her lips together, considering the man across from her who had just tucked a flower in her hair.

"Is that why you ran?" she asked softly. "Responsibilities, pressures, promises. Did you see your life stretching out before you like one big, long obligation?"

"Sounds like you're familiar with the feeling?"

"Answer the question, Walker."

"We're discussing McCormick here, not me."

Yet Savannah wanted to know, needed to understand why this man had left his bride at the altar. "You told me you loved her. Why did you leave that day?"

He looked out at the sea.

"You had a woman you loved, work you were good at, family, fortune. Everything. And you gave it all up? Why?"

"It only looked like I had everything, Slick. I didn't."

His eyes told her no more questions. She knew she'd overstepped her boundaries several questions back. But beneath his devil-may-care attitude and his bad-boy rep, she'd glimpsed a loneliness, a yearning. "What didn't you have?"

"Like a dog with a bone, aren't you?"

"What didn't you have?"

His lips twisted into a thin smile. "Not everyone marries for love, Slick. Let's just say, my fiancée was one of them."

"Money? She married you for your family's money?"

"Let's get back to you and McCormick."

"Security? Status?"

He chuckled in soft defeat. "Don't you ever give up?"

"Not when something's important to me."

"Well I know. But this isn't one of those important things."

"Yes, it is."

"Why?"

His question stopped her. Why was it so important she prove him not a scoundrel? Surely, with her wedding now only four days away, her attention should be focused on finding her fiancé.

"Because I don't believe you would have done such a thing unless you had a good reason. I don't think you ran to hurt someone else. I think someone hurt you. And you ran like a wounded animal."

She had surprised him as if she had discovered the truth. Gratefulness overtook his features before he vanquished it with a wry grin. "You would be alone in your theory."

"Walker, isn't it lonely?" She asked as she had this afternoon. Only her voice held no frivolity this time. "Always being a mystery?"

He pushed back his chair. "Are you ready to go find McCormick?"

She didn't move. "It must have hurt very much for it still to cause so much pain."

He dropped his head into his hands and groaned.

She put her hand on his. "Let somebody in, Walker."

He raised his face to her, kissed her hand, then removed it from his. "Believe what all the others believe."

"I won't."

He considered her a long moment, his gaze so intent, she couldn't have turned away if she'd wanted to. But she didn't want to. She wanted him to look at her like that as if she truly did fascinate him, as he'd professed not long after their first meeting.

"McCormick is a lucky man."

"Why?" she challenged, disconcerted by his gaze and the reckless currents rippling through her. "Because he ran? Or because I ran after him?"

"You choose."

"Is it so hard for you to admit you like me?"

"No harder than for you to confess your fondness for me."

She laughed, the deep, full laugh that had first come last night. He enjoyed seeing her shoulders ease, her laughter spill and reach to the golden lights in her eyes. They had sat too long, talked too much, and the connection that came only between a man and a woman had come to them.

He stood, reached his hand to the woman who was to be his brother's bride. "It's growing late."

Still she didn't move, only turned her face, devoid

of any playfulness now, to him. "Seven years. And there's been no one else?"

He didn't know how to answer her. Only stood helpless as longing and need deepened, filling him with guilt as much as wonder that this woman, his brother's bride-to-be, should be his desire. "Why does there have to be someone?"

"Because there does," she insisted in her dogged way. "That's the way it is. That's how the world goes round."

"Hah! Love. Look where it's brought us both."

Her face fell and he was instantly sorry. He pulled out his chair, sat down beside her. "No, no, you're right." He became the adamant one now. "That is the way it should be, but sometimes it doesn't work out that way. One loves more than the other. One loves not at all."

He waited until she brought her gold-brown gaze to his face. "But you go on, and one day, you wake and you think of their face and you feel..." He painted his own face with shock. "Nothing. No pain, no hurt, no desire. Nothing. And you wonder if you ever loved at all? If you had been mistaken? If that someone was not the one? If, perhaps, you will love another?"

She stared into his eyes as if hoping to see more. "It's not that I'm afraid I won't love again, Walker." Her voice was very small. "I'm afraid no one will ever love me."

"Savannah—"

She stood first this time, signaling an end to the

conversation. "Come. It's late. I have to call the hotels."

He could not move for a moment, knowing all he knew.

She squared her feet in their thin-heeled shoes. "I'm not giving up."

Something in his eyes, his expression must have made her hands drop from her hips. The fight left her face. "Haven't you ever wanted something so much, felt it was so right that no matter what, you would do anything to have it?"

He looked at the woman before him. He could only tell her the truth as he took the hand she offered. "Yes."

They walked back to the hotel, the night melting into the dark brilliance of the ocean. Each corner seemed to call with a new sound, a new sight. In the shop windows, Savannah glimpsed a high-cheeked stranger with a flower in her hair and a heat in her eyes. She turned away, startled at this woman. Herself. Still, the heartbeat inside her that had become too strong was not unwelcome. She would be wise to remember this moment, the woman in glass, staring as if she'd never been seen before. Maybe she would remember this most of all.

As they neared the hotel, she instructed Cash that she would call the hotels in the telephone listings under *A* through *N,* and he could call the latter half of the alphabet. She waited for him to laugh at her efficiency, and he did. What she didn't expect was to laugh, too, her methodic ways gaining a charm beneath the sound of their laughter. Until she remembered she was supposed to marry in four days, and she had no fiancé. She stopped laughing. They came to her room, and she hurried inside to begin her calls.

An hour later, she was at the end of the *N* listings and had not had any luck. She decided to see how Cash had fared. Still in her new dress, partly because she had little else to wear, partly because she'd never worn anything so flamboyant and she liked the way she looked in it, she padded down the hall. Too late she heard her door automatically click closed behind her and remembered that her key sat in the tiny purse on top of the television set. She'd have to call the main desk from Cash's room. She rapped on his door, waited, arms crossed, toes tapping the seconds, then rapped again harder.

"Cash?"

Several minutes of knocking and calling his name as loudly as she dared produced no results. She pressed her ear to the door, but heard no sounds within. He had either fallen asleep or gone out somewhere. She suspected the latter.

Why not? Had she really expected a man like Cash, reviled for his appetites and needs, to spend a night in a tropical paradise reading his appointed half of the telephone pages?

Funny part was she had, and now she felt strangely betrayed.

"It's none of your business what Cash Walker does. He's a grown man," she muttered, glaring at the locked door in front of her, then at her own locked door behind her. Drat. She'd have to go down to the front desk.

"He could've at least had the common manners to let me know he was going out," she grumbled, jabbing the elevator button several times. "Probably didn't want to listen to me nag him about it." Which is what she would have done, but that was not the point. "Coward," she declared as she stepped into the elevator, causing the other passengers to take a half step back from her.

She was crossing the lobby in her stocking feet, ready to do battle with the front-desk clerk should he even question her predicament, when she saw him. Cash. He was sitting in one of the many low plush chairs arranged in intimate groups around the lobby. A woman sat in the chair beside him. Her back was to Savannah, but Savannah looked at that cascade of thick, black hair and knew the woman was beautiful. Savannah touched her own crazy curls, sticky with spray. She was still standing there, staring, when Cash and the woman got up as if to leave. The woman's hair fell to her waist.

Savannah ducked behind the nearest cover—a large potted fern on a carved stand. She didn't want Cash to catch her and assume she was spying on him when she wasn't. Yet behind the cover of foliage, she watched. The woman turned, revealing a face, a figure that magazine empires had been founded on. She said something, brushing Cash's arm with her fingertips. Cash nodded several times, his attention undivided, as the couple crossed the lobby. Savannah decided immediately and irrationally she hated this woman.

"*Señorita?* May I be of assistance?"

Startled, Savannah spun around to the voice at her

shoulder, her stocking feet slipping on the marble tiles. Her arms whirling, she lost her balance, landing with an inelegant plop on her posterior in the center of the potted fern.

"Señorita. Señorita." The bellman came to rescue her.

She looked up from her graceless position and met Cash's puzzled gaze across the room. She saw the start of an amused grin. She decided she hated him, too.

"I'm fine, fine, thank you." She waved away the hotel employee and the others who'd stepped forward as she struggled to get up. She was brushing the dirt off her backside when Cash reached her.

"Looking for me?"

"Hardly." She blew a curl off her face.

"Admiring the local horticulture then?"

"I went to your room, and the door to my room locked behind me, and I didn't have my key, and you weren't there." Savannah's words tumbled, revealing her embarrassment. The gorgeous, caramel-skinned woman stood several feet back, watching them, her eyes full of secrets. Even Savannah's sister, second runner-up in the Miss Georgia Peach Pageant, would have been made to feel inadequate. Savannah decided she didn't completely hate this woman after all.

She turned her attention to Cash. "As you well know." Great. A touch of the shrew is always appealing.

"I came down to the front desk to try and get back in my room, saw..." She couldn't admit she'd seen him. He'd know for certain she had been spying on him and she'd feel an even bigger fool.

"Saw the wonderful design on this ceramic pot." She indicated the planter; the bellman was gathering up broken fronds scattered about it. She crossed her arms, considered the pot. "I'll bet it's handmade by local craftsman. Fabulous work, don't you think?"

He was smiling at her as if she were completely delightful.

"I bent down to see if there was an artist's signature and lost my footing, and well, you know the rest." She challenged him to question her explanation.

He looked at the plant. "Could have been worse," he consoled. "Could have been a cactus."

She wished to hell he'd stop smiling. With a significant lifting of her eyebrows, she looked coolly past his shoulder to the woman. "I take it you didn't find McCormick?"

"C'mon, we'll see about getting you back in your room so the plants can breathe easy again. I'll just be a second to say good-night to Apolonia."

Apolonia? Of course. What else would her name be? Her last name was probably Goddess.

"No, no. I didn't mean to interrupt anything."

"You didn't," Cash assured her and headed toward the woman. Savannah discreetly turned away as she waited for him.

"Scouting for more examples of Mexican art you can attack?" He teased as he came up behind her, his breath warm on her neck.

She faced him, saw the woman disappearing into

an elevator. "I'm going to see about getting my door opened." With as much dignity as possible she walked to the front desk. Cash waited while she explained the situation and got a new key. Together they walked to the elevators, got into an empty car. Savannah mentally counted the elevator numbers as they lit up one by one.

"For the record, it wasn't what it looked like," Cash said.

"You really have a grand opinion of yourself, don't you? Why should I care how you spend your time? Never mind the fact you were supposed to be in your room, calling hotels, looking for your brother."

"I wasn't the one spying, Slick."

She assumed a lofty expression. "I was curious. That's all."

They got off at their floor, headed down the hall.

"Although in this day and age," she noted, "you would be wise to remember casual relationships can prove fatal."

"So that's why you're marrying McCormick? He's disease-free?"

"The very idea." She marched toward her room.

"I'll bet you even had him tested."

She whirled around. "If you must know, that was McCormick's idea."

"You're kidding!" Cash's face lit up with amusement.

"We both had a test done. And you know darn well that has nothing to do with why we're getting married. I myself see nothing wrong with being pragmatic.''

''Not exactly a Hallmark moment though, is it?''

''McCormick and I aren't sentimental types. I say, better safe than sorry.''

''Now *there's* a sweet nothing to whisper in a lover's ear.''

She jammed her key into the door's slot. ''You don't have to get all ornery now because you struck out tonight.''

''Struck out? I did not strike out tonight. For your information, I didn't even go up to bat. But if I had stepped up to home plate, believe me, it would've been a home run. An out-of-the-ballpark, Mark McGwire-Sammy Sosa-Hank Aaron grand slam.''

''At least you still have your delusions to keep you warm.''

''You made sure of that, didn't you?''

She wrenched open the door to her room. ''Of all the ridiculous—'' She felt his heat. He was right behind her. A shiver went down her spine and the wild wings of anger turned to something else, something she refused to acknowledge. It was the late hour, she wrapped in rich silk, he too close behind her. She took a soundless breath, faced him. His nearness was overwhelming, his gaze intense. The shaky fluttery feeling spread to a dizziness. His face had always fascinated her, its ridges and angles, its texture. To touch it now would bring such newly-found pleasure. She stared at the lips she had kissed. A smoldering insistent need made her flesh tingle, her nipples pucker. He would be soft lights, she bet. Whispered sweet nothings, a single red rose on a pillow.

He touched the flower still pinned in her hair, her breaths light through parted lips.

"I'd forgotten that was there." Her voice was shaky. She reached to pull it out. Her fingers found his, tangled, went still. Everything went still, and she knew they were at the cliff's edge. One more step and they'd fall.

She felt heat against heat now. So much beautiful brown flesh. A strength and a vulnerability in those darkening eyes above her. She knew she could stop what was happening. One shake of the head, a single word. She wet her lips, suddenly dry. A low shuddering breath released from within him. They moved together in perfect harmony, two dancers meeting. He slid his hands into her hair. She raised her face to him, parted her lips wider, a soft cry of need coming from the back of her throat, becoming a helpless moan as he covered her mouth with his.

His tongue swept inside her, moving over and over in a primitive mating as he took her into his world. She'd been wrong. None of the proper, the refined, gentlemanly courting now. Only raw power, fierce unapologetic desire. Her body curved to him willingly, her flesh burning, and she cherished those clever hands touching her, stroking her fire, her heat until her skin seemed to strain and her spirit, base and belonging to him now, spiraled.

Clinging together, their mouths greedy on each other, they moved as one into her room. The door swung closed behind them. In the darkness, she let her hands see for her now, exploring the body that had drawn her from the first, touching everywhere, her frenzy frightening yet making her fearless. She had never imagined this degree of wanting, as if one's body was turning inside out where there was no thought, no reason. Only a guttural wail of need growing, urging, like a madness, and she a mad-woman, feeding off the flesh beneath her fingers as her hands roamed, slid over muscle and sinew and she sank deeper into a sweet ebony bliss.

She fell with him, laughing, onto the bed. He rolled her on her back, rising above her to look down at her in wonder. He lowered his head, pressing his face into the curve of her neck. She heard his breath hitch and knew he felt it too as the blood pounded through his body and desire pummeled all reason. His breath caught once more. He was as frightened and as help-less as she. She laid her palm to the roughness of his cheek. He raised himself on one elbow, his hand stroking the length of her slowly, gently now. Ah, as she had always known, there would be tenderness.

The phone rang. Her heart jumped, racing. She turned her head to it as if she'd imagined it. Both of them stared at it.

"It's late, too late" she whispered, hearing her own fear. Her body was trembling. She looked at the man above her.

He touched her cheek. "You should answer it."

"I know." But she only lay beneath him, the phone ringing, her heart thudding, the tick-tock, tick-tock of life so loud.

He rolled away from her onto his back, lay with

his arm across his forehead. She sat up, reached for the phone, but when she brought the receiver to her ear, she could not speak, could only listen to the voice so far away saying, "Hello? Hello? Savannah, are you there? It's me."

The weight of the bed shifted as Cash got up, crossed the room. The door opened, closed.

Savannah gripped the receiver with both hands. "Hello, McCormick."

Chapter Twelve

She tapped lightly on Cash's door, no longer bold. She knew he'd be up. She herself would not sleep tonight.

"Come in."

He was sitting in one of two chairs angled by the window, looking out at the moonlit beach. She saw his face and could no longer stand. She sat on the nearest corner of the bed, as far away as possible from him. "What a week."

His lips drew back in a soft smile that shouldn't have made her heart fall. "It doesn't count, remember?"

She remembered. They were her words. They were false when she'd said them. Her fingers twisted in her lap. They were false now. She still felt his touch on her skin.

He sat, all shadows in the half darkness and waited for her to go on. She spoke, his taste still sweet on her tongue.

"McCormick's at the lodge. He's flying out to Atlanta in the morning."

Cash's face revealed nothing.

"He left Mexico yesterday about an hour or so after I'd spotted him at the market. He'd tried to reach me, he said, called my office. They told him what I'd told them, that I was in Colorado at the lodge.

"He was going to fly up to Denver, but then decided to drive and check out several sites along the way on the border that the company had been considering for possible manufacturing operations. So the trip wasn't a total loss."

Her voice hitched in a sharp laugh that caused her to avert her face from Cash.

"When he got to the lodge, Mountain told him we were in Mexico, looking for him. Finally he got hold of your mother and found out exactly where we were."

She chanced a wry smile. "We were running around looking for him. And he was running around looking for us."

"You. He was looking for you, darlin'"

She turned away again as if she didn't want to hear any more. "While managing to scope out several feasible prospects for future production."

"Clever boy, my brother. He'll always do well."

She made herself face him. He offered her the kind smile of a compatriot.

"He's terribly embarrassed about the entire matter. Sends his apologies to you also."

"Begged your forgiveness, I hope?"

Her thin smile returned. "McCormick doesn't beg any more than I do."

"Pleaded for your understanding then?"

"Expected my understanding. I told him, yes, I understood. Sometimes, in unusual circumstances, we act out of character." Her gaze held his. "It happens to everyone."

"And it would not happen again?"

She did not know when the smile had left his face. Or hers. "Never."

"And you forgave him completely?"

A torrent of confused thoughts and emotions assailed her. What had happened to the level-headed young woman of yesterday?

"He didn't bolt at the altar, darlin'. He's still one up on me."

He was trying to make this easy for her. "No one's as rotten as you, Walker."

His smile came, told her she was a helluva dame.

He was wrong. "I never intended not to forgive him. I'm not exactly one to judge now, am I?" She looked at him, lost.

"It was a kiss."

It was more.

"A moment, that's all."

Was it? A week ago, it would have been a mistake. A week ago, it never would have happened. Now everything was different. She was different. She was to marry McCormick in four days. She looked at Cash, suddenly desperate for the answers that she'd always thought she had.

He folded his hands behind his head, leaned back in the chair, stretched out his long legs. "Spontaneous combustion. Over as quickly as it began. Afterward, nothing. That's all."

She didn't know if he was lying or telling the truth. Either way, she thanked him.

"Nothing but one night." He made sure she knew. "No wedding in white with all of Atlanta watching, no pillared Colonial on the north side, no skyrocketing career, no starring role in the social circus. One night. That's all I would give." Their gazes collided. "I'd be out the door before daybreak."

"And I would be hoping the door didn't hit you on the ass on your way out."

A faint smile touched his lips. "Clever girl, Slick. You and my brother, you'll be just fine."

"Fine. Just fine," she echoed.

"You will dance the 'macaroni' with me at your wedding this Saturday?"

She dropped her head. She didn't know pain could be so great. "I'd never liked to dance. Then, last night…"

Cash gentled his voice. "So your trip wasn't a total loss either."

She shook her head, not trusting the sound of her voice.

"Savannah…"

She had to stand, leave, move on. A woman—most of all Savannah Sweetfield—does not give everything up for one kiss.

"Promise me you'll keep dancing."

She closed her eyes and feared she had fallen in love with him. But when she raised her head, her voice was strong. "I will dance."

She stood. "I'm going to go, get some sleep." She was a liar. "I'll have to get to the consulate first thing in the morning. My money wire should have arrived. Then get a flight."

She made plans, felt the old self, the one in control and full of common sense, returning. She remembered the life she'd worked so hard to achieve, the life that would be waiting for her when she returned to Atlanta tomorrow.

Cash stood, but she gestured too emphatically for him to stay where he was. She couldn't risk him any nearer. She would not breathe freely until she was back in Atlanta. She said good-night and made her way out.

The door closed, and she was gone. Cash sat back down and found the night, searched for stars. He'd had wild times in his day, done crazy things. Some, not all, but more than most of the stories about him were made up or exaggerated, rumors that had snowballed from one source to the next. Yes, there'd been women, many women, although fewer as the years went on, and only those who, like him, wanted nothing more than pleasure.

There'd been brawls, too, but only if another struck him first or if someone needed defending.

Reckless times that seemed right when life had called to him with its brevity and its constant promise of betrayal, begging him to squeeze every last experience out of it. He had shunned the rules and mocked conventions, given and received pain as well as pleasure. But he didn't regret it. In his whole entire life, he'd never done anything he regretted. And he would not start now. He would not regret letting Savannah Sweetfield walk out that door.

THEY TOOK a taxi together to the airport where they would part. While she was going on to Atlanta, Cash was flying first to Denver to take care of some things. He would fly into Atlanta the day before the wedding. A collective sigh of relief had been sounded between the Walker and Sweetfield families at the news of McCormick's return, his intentions still intact. No one had doubted for a second that Savannah would patiently endure and, in the end, understand her fiancé's momentary fickleness. After all, she was the one who'd understood from the beginning, had told them all it was was a case of cold feet. A case now cured.

She stared out the cab window, the scenery blurred by the car's speed into melting colors and movement and light, a dream of itself.

Cash and she had spoken little. When they did, their talk was polite. Silence seemed to work best for them this morning. She pressed her forehead to the rattling taxi window, saying goodbye to this land where she'd discovered heat and magic.

They checked in at the airport. Cash's flight was later. He insisted on waiting with her until she boarded although she told him it was unnecessary. On the way to the departure area, he tried to buy her a soda, coffee, magazine, candy bar, a final shot of tequila as they passed the airport bar. She refused all his offers, but when the last one brought an amused smile to her face, he seemed to become content and sat with her quietly until passenger boarding was announced.

They stood at the same time and faced each other. ''At least you won't have to worry about losing your luggage on the way back to Atlanta,'' Cash noted as if searching for something to say.

She again wore slacks and a button-down blouse that had been bought at the hotel. The clothes Cash had bought her were packed away in a small tote.

''I guess there's a bright side to everything, even getting robbed.''

''Plus you've got a new anecdote for those family gatherings.''

She blinked too hard and fast. Time for her to go.

''You said you'd be married this Saturday and dog-gone it, you will. Gotta hand it to you, Slick.''

''Yes.'' She waited for the satisfaction she deserved to feel to come. ''You had your doubts, didn't you?''

''I was naive.''

He'd made her smile again. ''You've never had a naive day in your life, Walker.''

He thought of a day seven years ago. He thought of the last week. She was wrong. ''Born bad, that's me.''

She shook her head. Her solemn gaze never left his. They called her row to board. ''That's me.'' She dared to offer him her hand. He took it between both of his.

''I'd probably still be trying to find my way home if you hadn't come along and saved my narrow butt, Walker. Thank you. For everything.''

''You would've been fine on your own, Slick. Just fine.''

Just fine. ''And had a lot less frustration to boot.'' He grinned.

"But not nearly as much fun," she gave him.

They stood, hands clasped. She had to go.

"I'll see you Saturday then," Cash said.

"I'll be the one in white."

One more second, and he'd pull her into his arms and never let her go, damning all else.

Last call to board. He released her hand, pulled out a small packet of tissues, a roll of breath mints.

"Thank you," she said, too docilely.

"I'm sure the people sitting next to you will thank me more."

They stood awkwardly, not speaking. He leaned over, kissed her cheek. "Go," he told her.

For the first time in their relationship, she did as she was told.

"Cash?" She found him watching her when she turned. "This past week. It did count. It counted a lot."

It was all he would have. It was more than he would have asked for.

"I wanted you to know that." She was gone.

He stood at the window even after her plane could be seen no more. He laughed softly at himself. Who'd ever have thought he'd miss her?

NO ONE MET HER at the airport. McCormick had offered, but Savannah had told him it was unnecessary. She always took a taxi to and from the airport, preferring to leave her car at her complex's secured lot, and she would do the same this time. She was rewarded with relief in McCormick's voice. He was working frantically to get everything caught up before the wedding.

She walked to the line of cabs waiting in front of the terminal, automatically giving her office address as she climbed into the back seat. She needed to check with her assistant on the status of the wedding plans, meet with her team to get a full report on what she had missed while she was away. McCormick was not the only one who would be working at a break-neck pace to get back up to speed by the time the wedding rolled around on Saturday.

The cab pulled away from the airport, merging into the outgoing traffic. She watched as downtown came into view, would gradually swallow the cab, then her, whole.

The driver pulled up in front of her building. She stared up at the gray tower. She had rarely seen it from this perspective.

The driver looked at her over his shoulder.

"I've changed my mind." She gave him her home address.

SAVANNAH SPEED-DIALED, wondering if it was safe to talk on a cordless phone while immersed in three feet of hot, perfumed, bath-beaded water. She kicked at a bubble floating at the other end of the tub. *But oh, what a way to go.*

"Guess where I am?" she said, when the male voice answered on the other end of the line.

"Savannah." She heard contained delight. "My hope is Atlanta."

"Mmm. But guess where I am in Atlanta?"

"Savannah, I'm happy you're home safe and sound. How was your flight?"

"You're getting closer. Keep guessing."

"Savannah." A restrained patience answered her. "I can't wait to see you tonight as we planned, but if I'm ever going to get out of this office, I don't have time to waste playing guessing games."

"How come we don't have nicknames for each other, McCormick?"

"I see." Amused understanding came into the voice at the other end. "You took one of those tranquilizers that Doctor Kline prescribed for flying, didn't you? Remember what happened last time you took one of those?"

"I stood on my seat and sang 'Dixie,' naked except for the state flower of Georgia in my navel?"

"You fell asleep while I was speaking at the Rotarian dinner that night."

That hadn't been from the tranquilizer, Savannah thought. "C'mon. Guess where I am, cupcake."

"Cupcake?"

"Do you like that? I just decided that's going to be my nickname for you. Now you think of one for me."

"You went above the prescribed dosage, didn't you, Savannah?"

She blew out a breath, sent a bubble nearby spinning.

"Savannah—"

"You'll have to do better than that for a nickname."

"Darlin'."

"Not very original, cupcake."

"I'm really swamped here." McCormick attempted reasonableness. Savannah suddenly felt as though she was drowning in reasonableness.

"That sometimes happens when you go traipsing around North America."

"I understand." McCormick's tone took on a distinct distraction, and she suspected he had returned to reviewing reports while he spoke to her. "You're mad."

"Actually I called you up to invite you to come over and slip into my bubble bath with me. Does that sound mad to you, cupcake?"

"Savannah—"

"You're not going to think of a nickname for me, are you?"

"Savannah." An edge of exasperation slipped through. "I'm happy you're home, and I can't wait to see you and talk about everything, but I've got a ton of things to do right now, as I know you do, too. So we'll meet tonight as planned. My mother is expecting us around eight for dinner. I'll pick you up."

"I was thinking we'd have dinner alone tonight, just the two of us. Considering the past few days and all."

"You're so right. I couldn't agree more, but the wedding is in three days, and my mother needs to discuss the rehearsal dinner along with several other details, so you can see it just isn't feasible to waste any more time."

"Waste any more time?"

"Savannah, I know things are crazy right now and

that's all my fault and once again, I apologize but just remember, three more days and we'll have the rest of our lives together.''

Savannah set the phone down on the tub's tiled shelf. She stared at the silent receiver. "Bye, cupcake."

She sank back into the bubbles, took a deep breath of steam and lavender-filled air. McCormick was right, of course. She had a million things to do. She lifted her foot and pressed the button at the other end of the tub with her big toe, sending the whirlpool jets into action. She had to check and recheck each and every detail if she expected perfection to take place in less than three days. The bubbles rose, and she slid deeper down into frothy water.

Not to mention the stacks of reports and files and schedules waiting for her on her desk. She sank deeper. Then there was the fact of her stolen bags. She needed to apply for a new driver's license, didn't have a credit card to her name. The bubbles were tickling her nose. She hadn't even bought a new microcassette recorder. She slid beneath the bubbles, down, down, completely submerged.

"SAVANNAH, I understand you had limited means in Mexico, but, child, you're back in Atlanta now. We do have hairdressers." Her mother poked at Savannah's curls, hoping to smooth them into some semblance of order. "After all, no reason not to do the best with what God gave us."

Savannah tossed her head. Her hair puffed even

more, judging by her mother's stricken look. "I felt it was time for a change. I like my hair like this."

"And the dress?"

Amid the tasteful subtle blends of pastels, ecru, honey-gold, Savannah stood out like a house afire in the dress she'd worn her last night in Mexico.

"I suppose that's part of your desire for a new look also?"

Yes. Her desire. Savannah looked across the room to where McCormick stood with several of his fraternity brothers who were in the wedding party.

"Oh, never mind," Belle decided. "Why, when I think what could have happened, I have no right to fuss at all." She grabbed her daughter's hands and squeezed.

Savannah brought her gaze back to her mother's bright eyes. "You mean if the wedding had been canceled?"

"What else could I mean? Can you imagine the disaster? Not to mention the embarrassment. Not that it's been an easy task avoiding all the questions and innuendo this past week. But it could've been much worse." Belle leaned closer to Savannah. "No wedding, no merger—" she noted in a hushed voice.

"No merger?"

"Of course, no merger. Your father wasn't going to do business with someone who would embarrass our family so blatantly. Make us the laughing stock of Atlanta."

"No, of course not," Savannah said flatly.

"Fielding the questions this week alone has about done me in. But that's all water under the bridge, and here you are, sugar." Her mother again tried to smooth her hair. She clasped her hands to her daughter's cheeks, kissed her forehead, joy in her expression. "You're getting married tomorrow. Tomorrow at this time, sweetie, just think, you'll be Mrs. McCormick Walker."

Savannah shook her head, her curls accentuating her denial. "You know I'm keeping my own name, Mama."

Her mother rolled her eyes. "The point I'm trying to make, darlin' daughter, is McCormick and you are about to be married. Aren't you excited?"

"Actually, I'm feeling all kinds of emotions at this moment, Mama."

"Of course you are, honey bear. You're getting married tomorrow. Your father and I are so proud of you."

"Because I'm marrying McCormick Walker?"

"Well, yes. Of course."

"What if I wasn't marrying McCormick. Would you and Daddy still be proud of me, Mama?"

"Goodness, Savannah, don't be difficult. You always were such a moody miss at times. Oh, how I worried about what would happen to you. But I needn't have worried a fair hair on my head, need I, sugar? And you, so clever, staying calm when everyone else seemed to have lost their minds. But you were right. You knew it was only a matter of time before McCormick came to his senses and hightailed it back here before there were any ramifications."

"No marriage? No merger?"

"I swear, Savannah, you'd think for someone

about to get married…'' Belle dismissed her daughter with an airy wave of her hand. Satisfaction filled her features as she scanned the room. ''Look at this place, these people. One thing I'll say about Pauline Walker, she can be a bit snooty, but she does know how to throw a shindig—''

Savannah didn't hear anymore. Cash stood in the doorway, surveying the room, and the rest of the world went away. He must've just gotten in from the airport. It was the first she'd seen him since Mexico. Her first urge was to go to him. She didn't dare. His gaze found her, saw the dress she wore. He smiled. She smiled back, her hand fisting in the skirt's deep folds.

''There but for the grace of God,'' her mother's voice intruded. ''You could've ended up like that one's fiancée there. He's handsome, I'll give him that, but such a scoundrel. Running off the day of his wedding. Imagine.''

''Maybe he had a good reason.''

''What good reason could there be for breaking that poor girl's heart, shaming his family?''

Cash crossed the room to where McCormick stood. She saw eyebrows raise, the speculative glances as he passed. She couldn't answer her mother because she didn't know. All she knew was there must have been a reason.

McCormick embraced his brother. ''You finally made it.''

''I believe that's my line to you,'' Cash commented. Low enough so only his brother would hear, he asked, "Did you tell her about Apolonia?"

McCormick broke off the embrace. "Excuse us a moment," he told his guests, his gaze never leaving Cash. "My brother and I have some catching up to do."

The two brothers walked out of the room. Cash saw their father watching them as they left.

Cash waited until they were in the privacy of the library before turning to his brother. "She doesn't know, does she?"

"What would that benefit anyone at this point?" His brother demanded.

"Do you love her?"

"Apolonia or Savannah?"

"You shouldn't even have to ask." Cash sank down into a leather armchair as if weary. "I thought you came back here because you realized you loved her."

"Cash, I understand the disruption I've caused in everyone's lives this past week, and I am truly sorry but you don't exactly have the right—"

"Don't pull that reasonable crap with me." Cash stood, his voice taut. "I don't need the right, do you understand? I gave them all up years ago."

"Yes, you did, didn't you?" His brother's tone remained calm and cool. "The day you walked out on the woman you claimed to love. The day you walked out on your family."

"Don't try and make this about me."

"But it is about you. It's always about you. Seven years, Cash. Seven years, I've spent trying to do everything right, trying to make up for your absence, trying to live up to or live down the legend that was once Cash Walker." His brother paused. "You walked out on me, too."

"McCormick, I'm sorry…"

His brother shrugged off the hand Cash placed on his shoulder. "Do you think I meant to meet someone else? Do you think I wanted to fall in love only months before my marriage to another?"

McCormick got up, moved to the sideboard to refill his glass. He poured a fresh one for Cash. "I was in Mexico on business. I never believed in love at first sight. Bells ringing and birds singing and fireworks going off. Load of crap."

Cash took the drink his brother brought him.

McCormick sat down, raised his glass in a mock toast. "Until it happened to me."

Cash sat again. "She's very beautiful."

Anguish passed over his brother's features. "I was certain I had to be with her after I met her the first time. I came back from Mexico determined to call off the wedding. Dad said the decision was all mine. He only asked one favor of me. That I wait a month before I did anything to be certain I hadn't mistaken momentary passion for something else, something more. So many times, he said, he'd seen it happen. It could cost a man dearly."

Cash listened silently, his careful expression revealing none of the emotions, the memories he'd run from for so long.

"So I agreed, certain my feelings for Apolonia wouldn't waver. But there were so many other factors. The least of which was my engagement. Think what you want, Cash, but I do care deeply about Savannah. I respect her and trust her. We understand each other. It isn't such a terrible foundation for a future together.''

''Not to mention the guarantee of a merger between her family's company and yours.''

''I'm not proud of it, but, yes, that was a big consideration. The complete responsibility of the family business will be mine one day, and I don't intend to see it fail. A month went by, then another and another. And I was about to get married.''

McCormick scrubbed a hand wearily across his face. ''I thought I had made my decision, but as the wedding got closer, my feelings for Apolonia grew stronger. I knew it was wrong. I fought it for several days, went first to the lodge, thinking time away from everybody and everything would clear my head. But the only thing that became clear was I had to see her one more time. To make sure for myself, and for Savannah, too, that I wasn't making a mistake.''

He stood, poured another whiskey. ''I went to Mexico. She was gone. Her family never thought me more than another gringo seeking a moment's pleasure in Mexico. Considering my past actions, they had good reason. They wouldn't tell me where she was, but then a girl, Apolonia's cousin, came to my hotel, brought me word Apolonia wanted to talk to me, told me how to reach her. I called her. I heard her voice.'' His brother sat down. ''The wedding was only a few days away. It could have been cold feet. It wasn't.''

Resignation stole over McCormick's features. His

brother had grown into a man in the years he'd been gone, Cash realized.

"Apolonia asked for nothing except my promise that I be certain if I chose her, forsaking all others, I would be able to live in peace with my decision. She would be on the Riviera through Sunday. She would wait until then. If I didn't come by the end of the week, she would know my answer."

"She seems a wise woman for her young age," Cash said.

McCormick's mouth twisted into a faint smile. "Much wiser than me. I promised I'd take the time and think everything through until I realized that was what I did the first time. And it hadn't solved a thing. I checked out of the hotel, packed up the car I'd rented and was ready to go. I passed by the market on my way and decided to stop for some food, water for the trip. I parked, walked toward the market. It was a beautiful afternoon and I was in love. I swear, Cash..." His brother shook his head. "You should have seen me. You wouldn't have recognized me."

"You were wearing orange shorts. You were singing."

McCormick looked at him in surprise. "How'd you know that?"

"First finish your story."

"Yes, me wearing orange shorts and singing." He smiled now at the thought. "I must have been delirious."

"Or maybe just happy?"

"Yes, I was happy," his brother declared boldly. "I had made up mind. I would go to Apolonia."

"But you are here?"

"Yes, now I am here." A far-off look returned to the man's face. "As I said, I was walking, was almost to the market when I thought I heard someone calling me. Even stranger, I swear it was Savannah. Savannah calling my name clear as the day. At first, I thought I'd imagined it, but I heard it again. Her voice, my name. I was actually afraid to turn around and look. I left the market, got into my car, headed out of the city, but all that time I was hearing that voice, Savannah's voice calling my name."

McCormick met Cash's gaze. "I knew then. I knew I wouldn't be going to the coast or to Apolonia. Because I couldn't promise her the only thing she asked of me. If I made this decision, turned my back on everyone and everything I knew, I wouldn't be able to live with myself. I would not have peace. I heard that voice, Savannah's voice, and I knew I would always hear that voice, reminding me of the pain I'd caused to people I care deeply about. It was what Apolonia had feared. Now I feared it also. The relationship would have been doomed from the beginning."

McCormick smiled bleakly. "I envy you, Cash, but I'm not you. I made promises to Savannah, to my family. I can't just walk away."

Cash stayed silent. He could offer no defense. Let his brother think him a cold, uncaring son of a bitch. He would not be totally wrong. And the truth would hurt him more. Him and their mother.

"I went to Mexico to make sure I was making the right decision. Now I'm sure." McCormick rose from the chair. "It is for the best. The wedding will take place tomorrow. In a few months, the merger between the companies will be completed."

"And you'll be happy?"

McCormick released a short laugh. "Are you happy, big brother? You turned your back on everything and everyone to live the life many envy—no chains, no responsibilities, high in the beautiful Rockies, women as you please, good times without the guilt. So tell me you're happy, and I'll take the next flight to Mexico."

Cash saw the sudden plea in his brother's expression. He said nothing. He couldn't give McCormick the answer he so desperately sought. And he realized his brother might not be as wise as the woman he loved, but he was far from a fool.

"You'll be a good husband to Savannah?"

"I would not marry her if I thought otherwise."

Cash had no reason to doubt him. Despite coming close this time, his brother had never gone back on his word.

"C'mon." McCormick inclined his head toward the other room. "It's time we joined the others, have some fun. It's a rare occurrence when the infamous Cash Walker comes home, and I'm sure everyone is waiting for a scandal."

Cash stood, put his arm around McCormick's shoulders as they started out of the room. "And it's not every day that a Walker brother gets married. In fact, as most of Atlanta knows, so far it's been never."

Chapter Thirteen

The flutes began like birdsong. The violins followed, and the hum of voices dropped to the hush of whispers. Through a gossamer veil, Savannah watched her future in-laws go first, Pauline looking elegant in champagne silk, Franklin debonair in Armani. Their pace was perfect, their smiles charming, their head nods appropriate.

Her mother, resplendent in pale rose crepe, took the arm of her eldest, most handsome son. One by one, the rest of the wedding party followed, their beauty given by God, favored by youth and honed by money, modern science and formal attire.

Savannah and her father were left. The music, the flowers' perfume and a sudden still of anticipation surrounded them.

Jack cleared his throat. ''I suppose this is the moment I should have some fatherly words of wisdom.''

Savannah would have settled for an I love you, although she knew her relationship with her father wasn't of that nature. Their connection had always been the company.

Her father cleared his throat again. He preferred the

manly expressions of anger, impatience, scorn. Tenderness was something reserved for his wife in the privacy of their bedroom.

"You're a good girl, Savannah."

It would do. "Thanks, Dad."

"Do your mother and me proud."

It was all she'd ever wanted, she realized.

Her father crooked his arm. "Let's get this show on the road. After this past week, we wouldn't want anyone getting nervous."

She tucked her hand inside her father's arm. Together they stepped into view and were greeted by a collective intake of breath. They paused beneath the arched entry, waiting as the wedding march was cued. The flowers were lavish and lush, the white aisle cover strewn with rose petals. Candlelight flickered, adding its own soft radiance. Every face was smiling in anticipation and appreciation. She'd done it. She'd pulled it off. Everything was as perfect as perfect could be.

Then she saw Cash.

He stood, taller and darker than the groom, than any male in the wedding party, the wild recklessness of his beauty only cutting deeper in elegant black. She had spoken little to him last night, keeping her distance after the first sight of him had made memories and doubts rise with an alarming fierceness. Still, she hadn't pulled her hand away swiftly enough when it met his in greeting, hadn't protested more than a whimper in the back of her throat when he'd touched his lips to her cheek.

Now their gazes locked and she forgot who she

was, who he was, only knew the look in his eyes. The ivory orchids in her cascading bouquet began to tremble.

"Savannah?" Her father questioned, the natural command in his speech always strong.

Her gaze desperately darted to McCormick, seeking the crazy uncontrollable response that had not mattered before...yet now was all that did.

She looked at the man she was about to marry. She saw a good man, a man with a question in his eyes above his smile. But she did not find what she sought. It had never been there. Not for her. Not for him.

Her hand tightened on her father's arm.

"Ready?" he asked.

She nodded. The wedding march cued. Her father took a step. Savannah didn't move.

Her father turned to her. A murmur moved through the church. McCormick's smile became puzzled.

"Savannah?" Her father gave her a slight tug. She stayed rooted. McCormick's brow pleated.

"Savannah?" Her father's sharp whisper commanded her to do more than stand there like a statue.

She let go of his arm, lifted her hand and, as politely as possible considering the present situation, motioned to McCormick to come. The ripples rose within the church.

"Savannah, what are you doing?" Jack demanded.

She waved again at McCormick with his confused expression. The march finished. There was a silent pause, and the opening bars began again with a flourish, the musicians as confused as everyone else. The groom, the lines in his brow deepening, lifted his hand to stop the music. He took a deep breath as he started toward the back of the church.

McCormick shot a questioning glance at Savannah's father as he reached them, but Jack only shook his head and stepped away.

"Savannah, what is it?" McCormick took both her hands in his, stilling her shaking bouquet. She loved him more in that moment than she had ever loved him. And it wasn't enough—not for either of them.

He led her out of the others' sight. He faced her, held her hands and waited.

"McCormick, do I light the fire in your soul?"

He had the grace to chuckle. He was a good man. She would have been lucky to love him as he deserved.

"Savannah, a cathedral full of guests are waiting for us right now."

"Yes." She was ninety-nine-point-nine percent certain McCormick had already asked himself that question, or he wouldn't have disappeared last week.

"Savannah, you're a wonderful, intelligent woman. Any man would be out of his mind not to want to marry you."

She was not disappointed. It was the answer she had expected. "Do I light the fire in your soul?"

He rubbed the back of his neck. "This is about last week, isn't it? You're afraid I still have doubts about marrying you?"

"I'm afraid you don't have doubts."

"You're mad at me, aren't you?"

She squeezed his hands. "I'm grateful."

The frown lines stayed deep on his brow. "You're grateful I took off the week before our wedding?"

"If you hadn't, we both might have made a huge mistake."

"A mistake?"

"Do I light the fire in your soul?"

He finally considered her question. "Do I light the fire in yours, Savannah?"

She smiled at her friend. "I'd never even believed such a feeling existed."

He looked away. "It does."

"I know."

He looked back at her. "What made you believe?"

"Mexico," she uttered softly.

"Mexico," he repeated with the same hint of reverence.

She leaned toward him. "We deserve fire, don't you think?" she whispered against his cheek before pressing a kiss to it.

His smile was rueful, but relief flashed in his eyes.

"We would've made a great team," he insisted.

"We still will, working together for the new company."

"Are you certain about all of this?"

"Yes."

"Because no matter what, I'll always think I would have been privileged to have you as a wife."

"I agree." She grinned.

He drew her into his arms, planted a kiss on her forehead. She knew they would always be best friends.

"I guess we'd better go tell our guests," he suggested. She took the arm he offered.

"We both have some terrific sense of timing, you know that?" he asked as they started back.

"I suppose it'll be a real scandal."

McCormick patted her hand. "Don't worry. It's not the first time a Walker wedding has ended before it began and, believe me, this time, it's only half as bad."

SHE TOOK A last look at herself in the mirror. She smoothed the strapless satin bodice, gave a wiggle so that the full skirt swayed like any proper Southern belle's. Only a touch of sadness was in her smile as she looked at her reflection. Only a small sigh escaped as she reached her arms around, unzipped the back and stepped out of the dress. It crumpled to the floor. Finger by finger, she pulled off her long gloves.

Silence had greeted McCormick and her as they'd walked up the aisle to face their families and guests. Confusion had changed to disbelief on her parents' faces as she and McCormick had made their announcement. They'd apologized several times and thanked everyone for coming. She had avoided Cash's gaze, afraid he would see everything—the thoughts, the needs, the desires that had refused to be denied, and had demanded a decision.

She looked at her wedding dress in a heap on the floor. She was not sorry. She was not sorry at all.

She was on her way to her bedroom to hang the dress in an honorary position in the back of her closet when she heard the knock on the door. She had told her mother she needed time alone, although she knew it'd take General Lee's army to keep Belle away. Her mother's disappointment in her had never been overt, but Savannah, with the sensitivity shared by all children, had known Belle had always feared that her least-spectacular child would end up an embarrassment. Now that it had come to pass, her mother would waste no time arriving with alternatives and antidotes.

She could just not answer the door, but her mother's stubbornness had been the prime source of Savannah's own obstinacy. Rarely did either relent. Sighing, she slipped on the short tropical-print silk robe which was to have been part of her wedding-night ensemble and went to the door. On the other side was Cash.

He came in without invitation, gazed at her as if she were a rare and exquisite creature he could never hope to understand. She didn't know what to say. Especially now when there were so many things she wanted to tell him. She'd have thought she'd gotten used to him by now, the way he took her breath, made her fear, made her feel. She would never get used to it. Lord help her if she did.

She was trying to figure out what words to begin with when he stepped toward her.

She looked at him, helpless. "I decided I wanted one night."

She met him head-on, and in that interminable second before he fastened his mouth to hers, she wasn't certain she would come out a survivor. Then their mouths touched and she didn't care, didn't care for anything but this man, this moment. She took the sleek thrust of his tongue deeper inside her and became lost.

Her hands grasped his shoulders, pushing off the tuxedo jacket he still wore, pulling out the finely woven shirt until she found the flesh of his back, the hard ridges of his chest, wiry with hair, the pebbly circles of his nipples. With a delight bordering on lunacy, she drew in her breath, grinning gladly as he ripped off her robe, her back arching naturally to drive her breasts deeper into the strong lave of his tongue, reveling in the warmth and moisture and sensation far past sweet or sensuous. This was a rawness without relief, a pleasure-pain that swelled her pelvis as she reached for him and unbuttoned his pants. She had no need of foreplay. She'd had a week of foreplay and fun and games. She wanted them both naked and him inside her, fierce and full and thrusting until her head snapped back and her jaw locked and she split the physical limitations natural to them all and was no more than intense, excruciating, indescribable pleasure.

He took her there on the tufted rug, his hands working into the flat chignon of her hair until it came free, his fingers tangling in the strands as her body rolled and bucked and might not have been hers anymore but that of a woman possessed. His tongue took her mouth with equal, unrepentant demand as he plunged heavily into her, his maleness filling her without finesse or apology, but in a primitive celebration of man and woman bred into the sweet, full rush of their blood.

She bowed her back, rocked her hips, carrying him,

carrying them both. She could not breathe; she would not think. Her body reared up in a mad dance, crazed by the scrape of his teeth and tongue on her flesh. She feasted equally, her fingers clawing at his back, her lips taking to his skin.

Without breath or thought, the urgency that drove them both came finally, even then, in all its violence, not fast enough. And she was only flesh and pleasure and a completeness that nothing, no one, could ever take away from her.

He lay heavy on her, his labored breath hot and pleasing against her neck. Her arms wrapped around his head, holding him fast to her, not ashamed at her selfishness. Instinctively knowing it would only amuse and delight him, too. She tightened her thighs around him, lifted his head to bring his mouth to her again, draw his tongue inside her, wanting even more, the fires just ignited, burning too brightly. She worked her mouth to his, molding, learning the long sweep of his tongue, the smooth edges of his teeth. So much to learn. She wanted to know every inch. How much time would she have? Her tongue circled his and she pressed her mouth to his, unable to stop, fearful to end what she'd waited so long for, her whole life. She'd almost missed this; the thought caused her thighs to clutch. Her time would not be long. Even forever, it would be too brief.

Cash tore his mouth from hers, trailed it across her cheek, kissed the underside of her jaw, smoothed the hair off her forehead. She felt the tremble of his body, the effort he took to gentle his strength when there was no need. It was his fierceness she wanted. The unapologetic carnality. It was what she'd first glimpsed in him. It was what he'd promised her. It was what he'd taught her to crave.

His lips parted as if to speak.

She shook her head violently. She didn't want talk. Not now. Not yet. It was too soon for reason and explanations and expectations. The only sound she wanted was the rush of her blood, the gasp of their breaths. He looked into her eyes, she into his, and in the silence, they were joined.

She woke in her bed, in his arms. He was awake, watching her, and for a moment, she was shocked— at herself, at his presence beside her, at her gut reaction that she would lie like this beside him forever if she could.

She rolled away, sat up. She had not broken the rules without learning them well first. Still, after all this time, to find a touch that thrilled.

A fingertip traced the length of her bare spine and she thought no more. She lay back down on the bed, breasts bared, heart hidden.

He swept his fingers over one full curve, dipped his head to taste the offered dusty bud, the excitement inside her instant and excruciatingly lovely. She wove her fingers through his lush hair. He would ruin her for any other, she thought.

He kissed her neck, her nose and rolled off the bed. Sprawled and wanton, she watched the bare backside of him until it disappeared into the bathroom. She pulled the sheet round her, curled up on her side and settled into her pillow, content. She smiled when she heard the rush of water as the bath taps were turned on full force. She opened her eyes, saw the steam rising past the opened bathroom door. She closed her eyes, the small smile still on her face. It was a dangerous thing, his tenderness.

He came and gathered her in his arms, carried her into the bathroom to lay her down in lavender water, the late sunlight contrasting against the candles' fire.

"Caused quite a commotion today," he remarked casually, as if he weren't soaping her body, his hands, silky and wet, sliding across her breasts, her abdomen, the insides of her thighs. She grasped the edge of the tub, but still she was drowning.

"Yes, well, the aftermath will be worse, I suppose." Her voice was strained, gasping as his fingers dipped, swirled, took possession of her. She did not protest. She rested her head along the tub's back and closed her eyes, the water warm and silky all around her, and Cash caressing her. She made no sound at all until her hips rose, her body shook and her lips parted involuntarily, releasing a siren's moan of pleasure and fulfillment.

Not wanting to open her eyes, she found his hand and pulled until he splashed into the water atop her. She opened her eyes to see his laughing face above her, and even the abrupt thought that she had fallen in love with him could not dim her happiness.

He slipped beneath her, settled her on top of him in his arms, her back pressed to his damp chest, her body reclining across his. Their caresses became slow and deliberate as if determined to set the pace, slow the clock ticking incessantly. His hands languidly smoothed her skin beneath the water. In the cradle of his hard body, she rested her head in the curve of his collarbone and kissed the underside of his jaw, stroking his arms holding her.

"So how does it feel, Slick? Breaking the rules?"

She twisted her head to look up into his face, saw a concern he couldn't conceal. She wanted him to know there were no expectations. Even if there was nothing else but this moment now, she would have no regrets. "It was the right choice."

"Yeah?"

Her lazy smile took away any doubt. "Oh, yeah." Gratitude flashed in his eyes, surprising her. She had made the same mistake as others, thinking him invulnerable. She raised her hand to his cheek. He caught it, kissed the inside of her wrist.

She leaned her head to his shoulder. How long since she'd rested on another, allowed someone else's strength to hold her? She thought of her place in her family, her professional position, her past relationships. The answer was never.

"It was the right choice for McCormick, too." She raised up on one elbow. "One should marry for love, not duty."

"McCormick cared a great deal for you."

"And I for him, but he loves another." She smiled at her own lover. "I suspect she is in Mexico."

Cash nodded. He had gone to his brother in the church to make sure he was all right. McCormick had looked at him and said, "Apolonia said she'd wait at the resort until the end of the week."

"Through Sunday," Cash had confirmed.

"Wish me luck, big brother." McCormick had

slipped away while the others were still trying to sort out what happened.

Savannah snuggled on Cash's chest. "He's on his way to her now?"

Cash stroked her hair. "He is."

She nodded with satisfaction. "I'm glad."

"Savannah—"

She heard the name he rarely used, his serious tone. She raised her head. "This was my choice, Walker. One night."

His eyes took her in, and she feared she would waver.

"This is my choice."

His fingertip traced the curve of her cheek. His face had become too serious.

"You're not the only who can enjoy a good bout of rough-and-tumble sex, you know." She did not want him to entertain any worries.

"Angeline was my father's mistress."

She concealed her shock at the sudden truth, fearing Cash would retreat, go no further.

"She was not the first. I doubt she was the last, but I believe she was one of the longest. She was very young, and the affair went on over three years before Angeline realized my father would never leave his wife or her family's money. That's when she decided to say yes to her lover's son after several months of refusing his pursuit."

He paused, and she wondered if he would go on.

"I knew nothing of the affair. I doubt anyone else did either except for the primary players. My father's discretion has always been his strongest suit. I had

never been home much except in between being
thrown out of one school and being accepted at another after my father made a sizable donation. Finally,
however I had earned enough credits for a degree and
was expected home to take my place in the family
dynasty. Angeline and I met not long after, neither at
first knowing who the other was. All I know was I
took one look at her and was lost.'' His lips pulled
back. ''Like father, like son.''

''In the beginning, her refusal to go out with me
only added to the attraction and made me pursue her
all the more. The fact my father vehemently disap-
proved did nothing to detract from her appeal either.

''I learned the truth the morning of our wedding
day. Angeline had insisted it was bad luck to see the
bride the day of the wedding until the ceremony—''
Cash shrugged ''—but when have I ever been known
to follow the rules? I had had a diamond necklace
designed especially for her to wear with her wedding
dress, and I wanted to surprise her with it on the day
of our wedding. I heard them, my father and Angeline, inside her apartment, arguing. He was threaten-
ing her that he would tell me about their affair if she
didn't call off the marriage.''

His fingers, laced through Savannah's, tightened.

''When I confronted them, Angeline begged me to
believe that she loved me, that the affair with my
father had been a terrible mistake. She admitted yes,
at first, she'd been hurt by my father's lies and had
seen the opportunity for the perfect revenge in dating
her ex-lover's son. But she swore that then the last

thing she expected happened. She fell in love with me. The joke was on all of us.''

He was silent too long.

''You didn't believe her?'' Savannah prompted gently, saddened by the look in his eyes.

''To this day, I don't know if she was telling the truth or not.''

He stroked her damp hair. ''I wasn't as forgiving of my lover's betrayals as you, Slick. I threw the diamond necklace on the table and left. I didn't stop until I was a long way from Atlanta. They say they couldn't get her to leave the church that day, that she waited and waited.''

His voice took on a far-off quality. ''They found her still standing at the altar in her wedding dress the next morning.''

The bath water had gone cold.

''About a week later, she was killed when her car went out of control, hit a tree head-on.'' The remoteness in his voice wavered. ''They say she was wearing a diamond necklace. They buried her with it around her neck.''

Savannah wrapped her arms around him and knew he had never told the story of that fateful day to anyone before.

He looked down at her. ''My father hurt Angeline horribly, but it was my pride that killed her.''

''You can't blame yourself.''

''I am not without blame either.''

Her body to his, she pressed even closer as if to shed this skin and fall inside him, make him whole. She pulled his head down to her, sought his mouth and gave him the only thing she had. Herself.

Chapter Fourteen

One night turned into two, three, a week while the messages on Savannah's answering machine multiplied and Atlanta society was entertained again and again by the tale of the wedding that never took place. McCormick had made it to Mexico and hadn't returned. The gifts that had come prior to the wedding, not to mention the bridal shower presents, were waiting to be sorted through and returned. Two days after the wedding date, five hundred handmade glass hearts nestled in ivory lace intended for wedding favors, perfect for a paperweight, were delivered to Savannah's door. Meanwhile, both sets of parents of the ex-engaged couple were wondering whatever had given them the inclination to produce progeny.

Cash and Savannah finally surfaced on Saturday long enough to go to his parents' to gather the rest of his things. He was due back in Colorado by Monday. Savannah would drive him to the airport tomorrow. What happened next was anyone's guess. Savannah had spent a lifetime making plans, reviewing pros and cons, aspiring to ideals in an attempt to have it all— only to realize that if she'd married McCormick, she would have had everything except the one thing that mattered most. If her relationship with Cash was for only this past week, and the days before in Mexico, she would have no regrets. Regret would have been never giving herself to him at all.

"My, my." Pauline greeted the couple. She sat on the settee, a china cup balanced on her knee. She raised the cup and sipped from a gold edge. "Will coincidences never end? We just had a call from our other son south of the border, and now here you two are traipsing in. I must say, Cash, we don't see you often but when we do, things certainly have a way of getting exciting around here for the rare time my eldest son is in town."

"Pauline."

The iciness on the woman's face warned Savannah that familiarity, including the use of first names, had been revoked.

"Mrs. Walker," she began again, "if you're going to blame someone, blame me."

"Oh, I do, honey." Pauline sipped from her coffee, set it on her knee and gazed at Savannah with a cold-blooded poise that even now Savannah had to envy. "I do."

"Surely you've realized McCormick and I, we made a good team, but we didn't have, well, what my parents share or maybe what you and Franklin—" She saw the same hostility in Cash's father's face at her use of the familiar. "You and Mr. Walker share," she amended.

She looked back at Pauline, shocked to see an expression of such despair, she started toward the woman.

She'd only taken one step when the anguish on Pauline's face vanished so instantly and completely, it might never have been. Savannah glanced at Cash. He'd seen it, too.

"I suppose things could be worse." The elegant woman suddenly sounded defeated. "Lord knows they have been in the past."

"Mrs. Walker—"

This time Cash's hand on her shoulder stopped Savannah. She turned to him. His face was as void as his mother's. Except, his eyes asked for silence.

Savannah's gaze flickered to Cash's father. "Cash told me everything that happened seven years ago."

Franklin's eyes mocked her, daring her to speak further.

"What happened seven years ago isn't exactly a state secret," Pauline said. "On the contrary, there doesn't seem to be a soul left in the South who doesn't know the lurid tale of how Angeline Boudreau was destroyed by my son." Her cup made a sharp ping as she put it on its saucer. "After that ordeal, I suppose your and McCormick's little fiasco last week could be considered the comic relief."

"But—" The urge to say something in Cash's defense became stronger. His hand on her shoulder tightened, asking her silence. She met his eyes, saw his entreaty. Her body sagged.

"I'll go get my things," he told her, "and be right down."

She looked to Pauline and Franklin. Both were stone. "I'll wait in the car."

"WHY?" SHE DEMANDED as soon as Cash opened the driver's door.

He slid in beside her, gathered her in his arms and kissed her so deeply and completely she no longer knew where she ended and he began.

"You're welcome," she said when she could finally breathe again. "But I've still got a mind to march right back in there and set the record straight."

He cupped her face between his hands. "What good would that do?"

"Your mother should know the truth about your father."

"She does. Not the specifics like who or where or when. She doesn't care for details, but my mother knows there've been other women."

"And it doesn't bother her?"

"My falling in love with Angeline was an unforeseen complication, but as I mentioned, overall my father isn't foolish enough not to be the master of discretion. Appearances are important to both my mother and father. What I did seven years ago, what you did last Saturday—very indiscreet, completely unacceptable."

Savannah blew out a sigh. "I still say there's no reason she shouldn't know the truth."

Cash turned her toward the handsome house, the manicured lawns. "This is my mother's life, the world she created, the choices she made. Her husband was her choice also. My mother needs, now more than ever, to believe what she believes, that the choices she made weren't wrong. That's all she has left now. That's all any of us have.''

She turned into his arms. ''But your world was destroyed.''

''My world was never really here.'' He held her close to his heart. ''Until now.''

He kissed her mouth, then released her, and turned the key in the ignition. Savannah looked to the perfect facade giving no indication of the false lives inside. She thought of Pauline, the incredible sadness she'd glimpsed on the woman's elegant face. Good God, she realized, that could have been her. She closed her eyes, blacking out the image of wealth and success and happiness. She saw only the woman inside hanging on desperately to her illusions and wrong choices. That could have been her.

She looked to Cash. Whatever had been his world behind that brick front was gone forever. And suddenly she knew. Knew with the certainty of the abrupt loud beat of her heart. He would never come back here. He put the car into gear.

''Drive fast,'' she said with an urgency way beyond her simple need not to waste any more of the precious seconds they had before he left tomorrow.

Yet when the time came for them to say goodbye, it seemed the seconds had been too few. Savannah mocked her pledge, made bravely with her lover's arms tight around her, that a week, if that was all there was, would be enough. She looked up into the handsome face that still never failed to disturb and thrill her, and as she kissed him and shamelessly clung to him one last time, pride and promises to herself be damned, she knew a lifetime wouldn't be enough.

As CASH PULLED UP to the lodge, he saw Mountain on the porch, pointing out some peaks to three pretty gals who must have been part of the group booked from the east coast that arrived today. Fast-tracking, career executives who had traded their Jones New York and Donna Karan for the latest L.L. Bean for the week and come out here to remember pure air, untouched beauty, simple silence. He himself had known peace here at one time. Or had he only been hiding? He gathered his bag and slammed the door. Either way, Savannah had found him, and he had peace no more.

He saw the rapt expressions on the women's faces as they listened to Mountain, and Cash knew the man was spinning tales. He greeted the group, learned their names before going inside. As he moved toward the door, he spied a lone woman sitting in a rough-hewn chair far in the porch's corner, her fingers flying over the keyboard of the portable computer on her lap. Intent on the screen she was studying before her, she didn't notice him coming toward her until he closed the cover of the laptop.

"Hey!" Her head snapped up, her eyes flashing a fierceness he'd met before.

He held out his hands for the computer. "No laptops at the Lost Ridge Lodge, ma'am."

"I don't recall reading that in the travel information."

"It's in the brochure, ma'am," Cash just decided.

She leaned back in the chair and took him in. Cash knew at the same time, she was deciding if she should take him on. He smiled at the leggy redhead in front of him but thought of Savannah.

"It's Elayne with a 'y.'" The woman smiled back as she relinquished the laptop. "Elayne Mayer."

"Thank you, Ms. Mayer." Cash took the computer.

"It's the first door on the left upstairs. My bedroom." The woman's smile turned inviting. "For the laptop, of course."

"Of course, Ms. Mayer. I'll have Mountain bring it right up."

He turned away from the beautiful woman with the open desire in her eyes. Damn. Savannah had ruined him for life.

"How'd the wedding go?" Mountain found him on the back deck after he'd dropped his bag off in his room. He'd meant to go to the small room they'd converted to an office to check the mail that had come in his absence. But as he'd walked down the hall, the windows had called him and he'd found himself out here, staring up at the peaks as if he'd never seen them before. In reality he wasn't seeing them at all. His mind was too full of other thoughts.

"Not exactly as planned." His answer prompted a wide smile of satisfaction on the other man's face. "Savannah called it off."

Mountain grinned approval.

"Right before she was to walk up the aisle. She had a hold of her father's arm and everything." Now even Cash had to smile. Mountain grinned even wider with total satisfaction.

"Go on," he urged, his dark eyes merry. "Don't stop there. What happened?"

"You know what happened. You knew all along. You probably put one of your great-grandfather's ancient medicine-man potions in the salad dressing that night Savannah stayed here."

Mountain's smile spread to his whole face. "My great-grandfather ran a dry cleaners."

"Yeah, well, he still taught you all about herbs and plants and their supposed 'magical' properties. Probably put a spell on me, too."

Mountain kept grinning. "Nah, you're just in love."

Cash eyed him fiercely, then turned back to his beloved mountains. Maybe he couldn't openly commit to his feelings for Savannah, but he wouldn't betray them either.

"So, where is she?"

Cash stared at the landscape. "She's in Atlanta. Where she belongs."

"She does?"

"It's where she wants to be. Her job, her family, her birthplace, it's all there. Everything she loves is there."

"Except you," Mountain pointed out.

Cash ignored him. "And everything I want isn't there. There's nothing left for me there."

"Except her."

Cash sighed, turned to his good friend. "She's a

big-time executive in her father's company and she's damn good at it.''

"So were you."

"She wants the English Tudor with the wrought-iron gate in Tuxedo Park. Children, two or four—no awkward odd numbers."

"You don't want children?" Mountain asked.

"Of course I want children…someday, but she's put together this whole package—corporate career, society whirl, nannies, boarding schools, charity boards…"

He looked at his friend with appeal. "I'm not even sure where I'll be in six months, but I do know even if I could give her that kind of life, it's not what I want." He turned to the mountains. "I can't just expect her to give up everything and come out here so we can be together."

"Did you ask her?"

Cash shot a sidelong glance at the large man. "No."

"Why not?"

"I told you. I didn't want to put her in that position."

"That's not why," Mountain told him as he headed toward the sliding doors.

"No? Then you tell me why I didn't ask her to come with me?"

"You were afraid of what she might answer." Mountain left Cash to the setting sun.

SHE WAS JUST CALLING to make sure he got home safe, Savannah convinced herself as she dialed the phone that night. She'd been able to hold off until midnight but with the time difference she knew it wouldn't be too late to call Colorado. She was just concerned as any friend would be to make sure another friend got home without any incident, she reminded herself as the phone began to ring. That's what friends did. Except Cash and she weren't exactly friends. In fact, she didn't know what the hell they were at this point. She wouldn't allow herself to examine the situation and her feelings further.

Still she was embarrassed when Mountain answered the phone until she heard the pleasure in the man's voice.

"You've certainly had yourself a couple of weeks, now, if you don't mind me saying," Mountain remarked.

"I don't mind you saying, Mountain. I don't mind at all."

They chatted a few more minutes about the wedding that never was and what had been happening in Colorado since she'd visited. Finally Savannah summoned the courage to ask for Cash.

"He's not here, Savannah."

Everything stopped with those words except fear. "He flew home today." Her voice trembled. "He didn't make it up to the lodge?" Images formed of Cash lying along the side of the road, his ability to taunt the mountain curves with his speed finally failing him. She closed her eyes. They'd wasted so much time, so much foolish time when they could have been together.

"He made it up to the lodge, all right."

Savannah took a breath that seemed to reach her heart. Relief rolled in that Cash was all right; irrational anger at him, at herself followed.

"But he didn't stay put long. Took off after about an hour or so. Said he couldn't stay any longer, had to go, didn't know when he'd be back, if ever."

Running again. She shouldn't be surprised. She knew it was his way. At one time, she'd even envied him his fearlessness. Until she'd realized it was fear that kept him running. And even knowing this, she knew she wouldn't change him if she could. She loved him for what he was. Smiling through her tears, she said goodbye to Mountain.

SAVANNAH KNEW it was completely impractical to park on the street several blocks from her building, but she wanted to take in the breaking dawn a little longer, savor the last fresh air she'd probably enjoy until after midnight. She strolled down the street, her steps soft in deference to the sleeping city. Too soon she came to her building. For the first time, she hesitated before grasping the door handle. She pulled open the door, swallowing the small sigh that tried to escape. Cash had ruined her forever.

"Good morning, George," she greeted the guard behind the front desk. She leaned on the polished counter. "How'd Velma's surgery go?"

"Ms. Sweetfield. Now what are you doing here? Why, I thought you'd still be on your honeymoon?"

"So did a lot of other people. Including me. You must have heard the news though. The wedding was called off at the last minute."

"I'm sorry, Ms. Sweetfield."

"No need. It was a mutual decision between Mr. Walker and myself." She leaned closer. "Life, George. Just when you think you have it all figured out, it throws you a whammy and the fun begins all over again."

She straightened. "Well, guess I better get on with it. You have a good day now. Tell Velma I said speedy recovery."

She turned to the elevators.

"Ms. Sweetfield?"

"Call me Savannah, George."

"About Mr. Walker?"

"Cash?" His name came first to her lips now, not her former fiancé's.

The security guard nodded. "In your office—"

Savannah waved away the man's worry. "Don't give it a second thought, George."

"But ma'am—"

"Savannah, George, Savannah," she insisted. "Now don't you waste one more minute worrying about that matter." She stepped back to the counter, gave a wink. "Just between you and me, George, the man could charm the skin off a snake."

She got off the elevator, singing, "That Man of Mine." She stopped as she reached her office door, again hesitant. She hadn't been to work for a world's record of almost two weeks. As she unlocked the door, she couldn't even imagine what would be waiting for her on the other side.

The last thing she expected.

"You son of a bitch," she swore, moving toward him.

"That's a fine howdy-do."

"It's how I should have 'howdy-doed' you the first time I saw your arrogant ass in my chair." Christmas, she wasn't crying, was she? She was a complete sap.

"C'mon." He opened his arms and God help her, she crawled right up onto his lap. He kissed the top of her head. "You love my arrogant ass," he said with a softness.

She curled up tight to him. "I do, I do," she said with downright disgust. "I'm ashamed to admit it, but I even called the lodge last night. I'm sorry. I couldn't help myself. And Mountain said you were gone and I told myself I was okay with that, that I was okay with everything." She lifted her tearstained face to him. "What the hell are you doing here anyway?" she said, the fire that'd waited so long burning strong. "Haven't you tortured me enough?"

"Darlin'," His mouth lowered to hers. "I haven't even begun."

She kissed him back hard, and she didn't even care. The taste of him would take her forever to moonlit Mexican nights and glorious mountains and riding too fast for too short a time. She wound her arms around his neck, her hands curving to his crown and took her fill until when they parted, she was crying and laughing and breathless.

He reached into his pocket. She scattered kisses on his chin, his brow and every bit in between of that face too handsome for its own good.

"Here."

She sat back, looked up blankly from the small box he handed her, her mind still trying to deal with the fact Cash's rear, which she could now personally certify was golden-brown and as magnificent as the rest of him, was in her chair. At her desk. In her office.

She opened the box. Inside, wrapped in plastic, were several what appeared to be dark, dried-up sticks. She picked one up.

"Is this illegal?"

"Ginger root. According to Mountain, if you chew on it, you won't get motion sickness."

She sniffed the spice, wrinkling her nose. She cocked her head. "You came all the way back here to give me this. You must assume I'm going to be doing a lot of flying back and forth. Back and forth. Back and forth." She rocked in his lap, her grin wicked, and she without shame on this fine spring morning.

"No."

She stopped rocking. "No?"

He traced the curve of her neck, her cheek, his eyes following the trail his finger took. "I came to ask you to fly back to Colorado with me."

"And?"

He raised his clear green eyes to her. Gone was her teasing devil.

"And stay."

Her heart turned over. "Stay? For how long?"

"I was hoping forever."

Her expression became as still as his. "Don't mess with me, Walker."

"I learned that lesson over the last two weeks, Slick."

She bit her lip, but the small grin came. She tried to hide it by looking at the ginger root still in her hand. "Mountain says this stuff works, huh?"

She found a cautious smile on Cash's face and fell in love with him all over again. As she feared she would for the next twenty, thirty, forty years...forever.

"He seems like a very wise man, Mountain." She made her voice no-nonsense.

Cash's smile deepened. How he loved to taunt her. "He is."

She considered the wizened root in her palm. "And I only have to chew this? I don't have to smoke it or anything? 'Cause I'm not smoking anything."

"Mountain said you chew it."

Satisfied, she set the root back in the plastic with the others and closed the box's lid. She stared too long at the closed top.

Cash took her face between his hands, tipped it gently to his. "It doesn't have to be Colorado, Savannah. We can go anywhere, do anything, start right from the beginning."

His eyes locked with hers. "Or we can stay right here."

"Here? You'd come back here, to Atlanta, for me?"

He threaded his fingers through her hair, brought his face close to hers. "Wherever you are, I'll be there. I love you, Savannah."

"Stop. Stop." Her tears spilled over his fingers, but

she was smiling like the village idiot, too. "Stop making me cry."

He kissed her damp cheeks. "Say yes. And I promise I'll never make you cry again."

"Careful, Walker." She laid her hand on his face. Such a complex man. Take a lifetime to learn him. "Forever is a long time."

He brushed his lips across her palm. "Depends on your perspective, Slick."

"And what would your perspective be, Walker?"

He rested his brow to hers. "It won't be long enough."

"No…"

His gaze searched hers. Her heart thudded. She stretched to kiss his mouth.

"It won't nearly be long enough," she whispered as her lips found his.

HARLEQUIN®

AMERICAN *Romance*®

celebrates twenty years!

Look who's celebrating with us:

Beloved author
JUDY CHRISTENBERRY
graces the lineup with her compelling novel,

Saved by a Texas-Sized Wedding
May (HAR #969)

Don't miss this delightful addition
to the popular series **Tots for Texans**

It's a marriage-of-
convenience story that
will warm your heart!

And in June, from **Cathy Gillen Thacker,** watch for
a brand-new title in **The Deveraux Legacy** series.

Available at your favorite retail outlet.

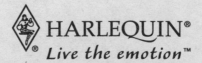

HARLEQUIN®
Live the emotion™

Visit us at www.eHarlequin.com

HAR20JC

HARLEQUIN®

AMERICAN *Romance*®

Celebrating 20 Years
of home, heart and happiness!

As part of our yearlong 20th Anniversary celebration, Harlequin American Romance is launching a brand-new cover look this April. And, in the coming months, we'll be bringing back some of your favorite authors and miniseries. Don't miss:

THAT SUMMER IN MAINE
by Muriel Jensen

A heartwarming story of unexpected second chances, available in April 2003.

SAVED BY A TEXAS-SIZED WEDDING
by Judy Christenberry

Another story in Judy's bestselling *Tots for Texans* series, available in May 2003.

TAKING OVER THE TYCOON
by Cathy Gillen Thacker

A spin-off story from Cathy's series, *The Deveraux Legacy*, available in June 2003.

We've got a stellar lineup for you all year long, so join in the celebration and enjoy all Harlequin American Romance has to offer.

 Available at your favorite retail outlet.

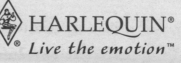
HARLEQUIN®
Live the emotion™

Visit us at www.eHarlequin.com

HARTAC2

eHARLEQUIN.com

Sit back, relax and enhance your romance
with our great magazine reading!

- **Sex and Romance!** Like your romance
  hot? Then you'll *love* the sensual reading
  in this area.

- **Quizzes!** Curious about your lovestyle?
  His commitment to you? Get the
  answers here!

- **Romantic Guides and Features!**
  Unravel the mysteries of love with
  informative articles and advice!

- **Fun Games!** Play to your heart's content....

**Plus...romantic recipes,
top ten lists,
Lovescopes...and more!**

**Enjoy our online magazine today—
visit www.eHarlequin.com!**

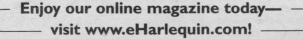

INTMAG